'A prospective lover should make an impression,' Ramon told Noreen. 'He should make you tremble with delicious, forbidden thoughts and longings. He should leave you flushed with the force of your need for him. It should give you pleasure just to look at him. You show none of these signs when your friend, Donaldson, visits.'

His eyes narrowed on her flushed face, and he noted the slight tremor of her hands when they touched the sheet covering her. 'I don't think you love him,' he added bluntly.

'I like him…very much,' she protested.

'He isn't the man for you. He doesn't leave you shaken and flushed when he comes out of your room.'

She clenched her teeth and glared at him. 'I'm cold,' she said doggedly. 'And I think I have a fever!'

'A fever for me?'

Dear Reader,

LET'S CELEBRATE FIFTEEN YEARS OF SILHOUETTE DESIRE®...

...with some of your favourite authors and new stars of tomorrow. May's MAN OF THE MONTH is the simply irresistible Ramon Cortero, in an eagerly awaited **Diana Palmer** story, *The Patient Nurse*. Next month's MAN OF THE MONTH title is from Ann Major, so don't miss that, either!

This month also sees the start of an exciting new mini-series ALWAYS A BRIDESMAID!—where five couples say 'I do' with a little help from their friends. The first book is *The Engagement Party* by Barbara Boswell; we're sure you'll love all of them. *The Bridal Shower* by Elizabeth August is in Desire™ next month, and then there's one a month in every other Silhouette® series.

Next, sexy Joe Camden gets a surprise mail-order family in Raye Morgan's fantastic *Wife by Contract*, and then for a really sexy story, meet wild Jed Ryder in *The Midnight Rider Takes a Bride* by Christine Rimmer. And Amy Fetzer brings us her first romance, *Anybody's Dad*; it's a story concerning parenthood—with a twist. Finally, if you're looking for fun and frolics—and a high dose of sensuality—don't miss Patty Salier's latest, *The Honeymoon House*.

Enjoy these celebration books and may we have many more years of happy reading together!

The Editors

DIANA PALMER

The Patient Nurse

SILHOUETTE

Desire®

*First published in Great Britain 1998
Silhouette Books, Eton House, 18-24 Paradise Road,
Richmond, Surrey TW9 1SR*

© Diana Palmer 1997

ISBN 0 373 76099 X

22-9805

*Printed and bound in Great Britain
by Mackays of Chatham PLC, Chatham*

To doctors and nurses
and hospitals everywhere.

One

He heard the whispered, amused comments as he walked down the hall toward the cardiac care unit of St. Mary's Hospital, and it was hard work not to grin. He'd just been interviewed on local television that morning about his habits in the operating room. The interviewer had elicited the information that Dr. Ramon Cortero liked to listen to the rock group Desperado while he performed the open-heart surgery that he was world-famous for. The nurses and technicians in the cardiac ward where he worked had teased him about it affectionately all day. They were a team, he and these hardworking people, so he didn't take offense at the teasing. In fact, some of them were fans of the Wyoming-based group Desperado as well.

His black eyes danced in a lean and darkly handsome face as he strode along in his surgical greens, scouting for the wife of a patient in whom he'd just replaced a malfunctioning heart valve.

The woman wasn't where she was supposed to be—in the surgical waiting room on the second floor. The CCU nurse had inadvertently sent her down to the main lobby waiting room, and when he'd phoned down there, she was missing. She was a middle-aged woman whose husband had survived against the odds, having been brought in with a leaky prosthetic valve complicated by pneumonia. It had taken all Ramon's skill, and a few prayers, to bring the man through it. Now he had good news for this woman, if he could find her.

The elevator doors opened nearby, and when he turned, there she was, surrounded by her teenage son, in a long black coat, several members of her husband's family, and one of the female chaplains who'd rarely left her side since the ordeal began forty-eight hours earlier. She looked her age. Her eyes were red and puffy from much crying, and there was a desperate plea in them.

Ramon smiled, answering the question she seemed afraid to ask. "He came through just fine," he said without preamble. "He has a strong heart."

"Oh, thank God," she whispered, and hugged her son. "Thank God! And thank you, Doctor." She extended a hand and shook his hand.

"*De nada,*" Ramon said with a gentle smile. "I'm glad we could help him."

The cardiologist, a debonair African-American, grinned from his stance near the heart surgeon. It was he who had met the woman and her son at the door as they arrived in the critical care unit and explained the heart catherization procedure as well as the valve replacement surgery to them. It was he who'd offered comfort and a glimmer of hope. The woman shook hands with him and smiled broadly, adding her thanks to him as well.

Dr. Ben Copeland only shrugged. "That's what we're here for," he said, and smiled back. "Your husband is in the intensive care unit just down this hall. There's a room next to it where you can wait until he's hooked up to the monitors, and then you can see him."

There were more thanks, more tears. A nurse came along and was dispatched to show the relieved family where they could wait until they were allowed to see the patient.

Ben joined Ramon. "Sometimes," he said, "we have miracles. I wouldn't have bet a cup of coffee on that man's chances when he was brought in."

"Neither would I," Ramon agreed grimly. "But sometimes we get very lucky indeed." He sighed and stretched. "I could sleep for a week, but I'm still on call. I guess you get to go home."

Ben grinned.

"Lucky devil." He shook his head and left the other man with a wave of his hand as he went to check on the other two surgical patients he'd managed, with God's help, to pull back from the abyss. There had been three emergency surgeries on this otherwise quiet Sunday when he was on call. He was stiff and sore and very tired. But it was a good sort of tired. He paused at a window to gaze with quiet satisfaction at the huge lighted cross on the main hospital wall. Prayers were often answered. His had been tonight.

He checked his patients, wrote out the orders,

dressed and went over to O'Keefe City Hospital across the street to visit three other new patients on whom he'd performed surgery. He also had to go to Emory University Hospital in Decatur on the way home to check a patient there who was ready to be dismissed. All his rounds made, he went home.

Alone.

His apartment was spacious, but not outwardly the home of a wealthy man. He preferred simplicity, a holdover from his childhood in Havana, in the barrio. He picked up a copy of Pio Baroja's *Cuentos* and smiled sadly. There was an inscription just inside the cover that he knew by heart. "To Ramon from Isadora, with all my love." His wife, who had died of pneumonia, of all things, only two years before. She had died while he was abroad performing complicated bypass surgery on a very important diplomat. She had died because of neglect, because her cousin had left her alone all night and the fluid in her lungs, combined with a desperately high fever, had killed her.

It was ironic, he thought, that he hadn't been home the one time he was truly needed. He'd left Isadora with her young cousin, Noreen, a registered nurse. He'd thought he could trust Noreen to take care of her. But she'd left Isadora, and when Ramon came home from overseas, it was to find her already gone, already beyond the reach of his arms. He'd blamed, still blamed, Noreen for her neglect. She'd tried desperately to explain, but he'd refused to listen. Wasn't her sin apparent to everyone, even to her aunt and uncle, who had blamed her as vehemently as he had?

He put the book down, running his fingers lovingly over the cover. Baroja, a famous Spanish novelist of the early twentieth century, had been a physician as well as an author. He was Ramon's favorite. The stories in this collection were full of Baroja's life in the barrio of Madrid before antibiotics were discovered. They were stories of pain and tragedy and loneliness, and through it all, hope. Hope was his stock-in-trade. When all else failed, there was still faith in a higher power, hope that a miracle could occur. One had occurred tonight, for that lady whose husband was in ICU. He was glad, because it was a good marriage and those people were in love, as he and Isadora had been. At the beginning, at least...

He sighed and turned toward the kitchen. He opened the refrigerator.

"Ay, ay, ay," he murmured softly to himself as he surveyed the contents. "You're a world-famous cardiac surgeon, Señor Cortero, and tonight for your supper you will feast on a frozen dinner of rubber chicken and undercooked broccoli. How the mighty have fallen!"

The sudden ringing of the telephone brought his head, and his eyebrows, up. He was still technically on call until midnight, and he might be needed.

He lifted the receiver. "Cortero," he said at once.

There was a pause. "Ramon?"

His face hardened. He knew the voice so well that only two syllables gave away its identity over the telephone.

"Yes, Noreen," he said coldly. "What do you want?"

There was a hesitation, also familiar. "My aunt wants to know if you're coming to my uncle's birthday party." How stilted those words. She and her aunt and uncle weren't close. They never had been, but the distance was especially noticeable since Isadora's death.

"When is it?"

"You know when."

He sighed angrily. "If I'm not on call next Sunday, I'll come." He toyed with a slip of paper on the spotless glass-topped telephone table. "Are you going to be there?" he added darkly.

"No," she said without any trace of feeling in her voice. "I took his present over today. They'll be out of town until the weekend, so they asked me to call you."

"All right."

There was another pause. "I'll tell my aunt that you're coming." She hung up.

He put the receiver down and pressed it there. It felt cold under his fingers, cold like the inside of his heart where Isadora was. He could never separate the memory of her death from Noreen, who could have saved her if she'd been at home. It was unreasonable, this anger. He realized that, on some level. But he'd harbored his grudge, fed it on hate, fanned the flames to thwart the pain of losing Isadora in such a way. He made himself forget that Noreen had loved Isadora, that her grief had been every bit as genuine as his own. He hated her and couldn't hide it. Hating Noreen was his solace, his comfort, his security.

To give her credit, she never accused him of being unjust or unreasonable. She simply kept out of his way. She worked in O'Keefe City Hospital across the street from St. Mary's, where he performed most of his surgeries. She was one of two registered nurses who alternated night duty on a critical care ward. Sometimes he had patients in her unit, whom he had to visit on rounds. But he treated her even there as a nuisance. She had a university degree in nursing science. She had the talent and intelligence to become a doctor, but for some reason, she'd never pursued such a career. She'd never married, either. She was twenty-five now, mature and levelheaded, but there were no men in Noreen's life. Just as there were no women in Ramon's.

He went back into the kitchen and made himself a pot of coffee. He required very little sleep, and his work was his life. He wondered what he would have done without it since losing Isadora.

He smiled, remembering with sad poignancy her elegant blond beauty, those vivid blue eyes that could smile so warmly. Noreen was a poor carbon copy of her, with dishwater blond hair and gray eyes and no real looks to speak of. Isadora had been beautiful, a debutante with exquisite poise and manners. The family was very wealthy. Noreen shouldn't have to work at all, because she was the only surviving heir to the Kensington fortune. But she had apparently little use for money, because even when she was off duty, she seemed to dress down. She had an apartment and never asked her aunt and uncle for a penny to help support her. He wondered what their response would have been if she had asked, and was amazed that he concerned himself with her at all.

Noreen had been a puzzle since he'd met Isadora, six years before. Isadora was outgoing and gregarious, always flirting and fun to be with. Noreen had been very quiet, rarely exerting herself. She'd had no social life to speak of. She was studious and reserved back then, a nurse in training, and her profession seemed to be paramount in her life.

Ramon frowned. Odd, he thought, how a woman so wrapped up in nursing could have been so negligent with her own cousin. Noreen was so conscientious on the ward that she was often reprimanded for questioning medicine orders that seemed unacceptable to her.

Perhaps she'd been jealous of Isadora. Still, why would she have gone so far as to leave a critically ill woman alone in an apartment for almost two nights?

One of his colleagues had mentioned Noreen to him shortly after the funeral, and remarked how tragic the whole business was, especially Noreen's condition. He'd snapped that Noreen was no concern of his and walked off. Now he wondered what the man had meant. It was a long time ago, of course. The colleague had long since moved to New York City.

He dismissed the thought from his mind. God knew, he had more important things to think about than Noreen.

That Sunday afternoon, since he wasn't on call, he did go to see Hal Kensington, Isadora's father, bearing a birthday present—a gold watch. Mary Kensington met him at the door, soignée in a leopard-striped silk caftan with her platinum blond hair, so much like Isadora's, in a neat bun atop her head.

"Ramon, how sweet of you to come," she said enthusiastically, taking his arm. She made a face. "I'm sorry I had to ask Noreen to phone you about today. I knew I'd never have time to run you down, with all my charity work, you know."

"It's all right," he said automatically.

She sighed. "Noreen is a cross that we must all

bear, I'm afraid. Fortunately we don't see her except at Christmas and Easter, and only then at church.''

He glanced down at her curiously. "You raised her.''

"And I should feel something for her, you think.'' Mary laughed without humor. "She was Hal's only brother's child, so we were obligated to take her in when her parents died. But it wasn't from choice. She was always in the way. She's going to be an old maid, you know. She dresses like someone out of the local shelter and as for parties, my dear, I never invite her for them, she's so depressing! She was always like that, even as a child. Isadora was so different, so sweet, so loving. She was our whole world from the minute she was born. Of course, Noreen stayed with my mother a great deal of the time, until her death.'' She glowered. "Noreen was a burden. She still is.''

How strange that he should feel a twinge of pity for the sad little girl who came to live with people who didn't want her.

"Don't you love Noreen?'' he asked bluntly.

"My dear, who could love such a pale shadow of a woman?'' she asked indifferently. "I suppose I'm fond of her, but I can never forget that she cost us our Isadora. As I'm sure you can't,'' she added, patting his arm comfortingly. "We all miss her so much.''

"Yes,'' he said.

Hal was sprawled in his favorite easy chair, his bald head reflecting the light from the crystal chandelier overhead. He looked up from the yachting magazine he was reading as the other two joined him.

"Ramon! So glad you could come!'' He put the

magazine aside and stood up to shake hands warmly with his son-in-law.

"I brought you a little something," he said, handing Hal the elegantly wrapped package.

"How kind." Hal beamed. He opened it and enthused over the watch. "Just what I wanted," he said. "I have a sport watch, but I can wear this one to the yacht club. Thanks!"

Ramon waved the thanks away. "I'm glad you like it."

"Noreen gave him a wallet," Mary said disparagingly.

"Eel skin," Hal added, shaking his head. "The girl has no imagination."

Ramon remembered where Noreen lived, the clothes she wore off duty. She apparently had little money, since she asked for nothing from her aunt and uncle, and eel skin wallets were expensive. He wondered what she might have gone without to buy her uncle that present, about which he was so cavalier. Ramon knew what it was to be poor. He was grateful for any gift he received, however meager.

He recalled that Noreen had chosen a small crystal bud vase for Isadora as a wedding gift when they married. Isadora had tossed it aside without a care, much more enthusiastic about the Irish linen tablecloth that a girlfriend had brought her. Noreen hadn't said a word, but a male nurse who had accompanied her to the engagement shower remarked loudly that Noreen had gone without a badly needed coat to buy that elegant trifle for her unappreciative cousin. Isadora had heard him, red-faced, and immediately picked up the bud vase and made a fuss over it. But it was too late. Noreen had held her head up proudly, never shed a tear. But her eyes had been so sad…

"Are you listening, Ramon?" Hal murmured. "I said, we'll have to go sailing one weekend."

"I'd like that, when I have time," Ramon replied, but without enthusiasm. He was uncomfortable with these people. They picked their friends by their bank balances and social position. Ramon had been acceptable because he was famous and well-to-do. But the Ramon Cortero who had escaped from Cuba with his parents at the age of ten wouldn't have been welcomed as a prospective in-law. He knew it, now more vividly than ever. Odd, these disjointed thoughts that plagued him lately.

He stayed only long enough for cake and coffee, served on the finest china, and then excused himself. Outside, he looked back at the large brick mansion with no real feeling at all. The house was as bland and indifferent as the people who lived inside it. He wondered what was happening to him to make him feel so uncomfortable with Isadora's parents, who had been so kind to him after her death.

He drove himself back to his apartment in the silver Mercedes that was his pride and joy. He couldn't remember feeling so empty since the funeral. Probably he was overtired and needed a vacation. He should take a week off, just for himself, and go away. He could fly down to the Bahamas and laze on the beach for a few days. That might perk him up.

He glanced around him at the beautiful city skyline, ablaze with colorful lights, and remembered how that elegant glitter used to remind him of beautiful Isadora. She was sweetness itself to him, but he remembered vividly walking in on her once when she was cursing Noreen like a sailor for not putting her sweaters in the right drawer. Noreen hadn't said a word in her own defense. She'd rearranged the clothes and left the room, not quite meeting Ramon's eyes.

Isadora had laughed self-consciously and murmured that good help was just so hard to find. He'd thought it a cold remark for a woman to make about her own cousin, and he'd said so. Isadora had laughed it off. But he'd watched, then, more closely. Isadora and her parents treated Noreen much more like a servant than like a member of the family. She was always fetching and carrying for someone, making telephone calls, arranging caterers and bands for parties, writing out invitations. Even when she was studying for exams, the demands from her family went on without pause.

Ramon had remarked once that exams called for a lot of study, and the other three Kensingtons had looked at him with blank faces. None of them had ever gone to college and had no idea what he was talking about. Noreen's duties continued without mercy. It wasn't until she left home, just after Isadora's marriage, that the Kensingtons hired a full-time housekeeper.

He went back to his apartment and made himself a cup of coffee. It disturbed him that he should think of Noreen so much, and especially on her uncle's birthday. There had been parties for Hal, and Mary Kensington before, but Noreen had rarely been included in the celebrations. It was as if her presence in the family was forgotten until something needed doing that only she could do, such as nursing Isadora through flu and colds and nuisance ailments.

That reminded him of Isadora's pneumonia and

Noreen's neglect, and he grew angry all over again. Despite his wife's faults, he'd loved her terribly. Even though Noreen had been badly treated by her aunt and uncle and cousin, it was no excuse to let Isadora die. He might feel pity for her lack of love, but he still felt only contempt when he remembered that Isadora had died because of her.

He spent six days in the Bahamas, alone, enjoying the solitude of the remote island where he had a room in a bed-and-breakfast inn. He'd walked along the beach and remembered painfully the happy days he'd spent here with Isadora on their honeymoon. He still missed her, despite their turbulent relationship.

He noticed gray hairs now and felt his age as never before. He should remarry; he should have a son. Isadora hadn't wanted children and he hadn't pressed her about it. There had been plenty of time. Or so he thought.

The sunset was particularly vivid, as if it were a canvas worked by a madman in fiery colors with black highlights, slicing down to the horizon like a bloody knife. He sighed as he stared at it and listened to the sweet watery whisper of the surf near his bare feet. How poignant, to hold such sights in the heart and have no one to share them with. He was alone. How he longed for a loving wife and plenty of children playing around him on the beach. Perhaps it was time he started thinking of the future instead of the past. Two years was surely long enough to mourn.

He went back to work with a vengeance, taking on a bigger workload than ever before as time passed. He was operating on a private patient at O'Keefe City

Hospital, across the street from St. Mary's. It was just after a particularly rough operation that he was called to the cardiac care ward to check a patient the night nurse wasn't too happy about. He had three patients in this hospital, in addition to patients at St. Mary's and Emory.

He wasn't happy when he discovered who the night nurse was. Noreen, in her usual white slacks and colorful long jacket, with a stethoscope around her neck, her hair in a bun, gave him a cool look as he paused at the circular nurses' station.

"I didn't think this was the night you worked at O'Keefe," he said shortly, still in his surgical greens.

"I work whenever I have to, and what are you doing at O'Keefe?" she asked.

"I had a patient who requested that his surgery be performed here. I'm on staff at three hospitals. This is one of them," he replied, equally coldly.

"I remember," she said. Her hands went into the pockets of her patterned jacket. "Your Mr. Harris is throwing up. He can't keep his medicine down."

"Where's his chart?"

She went to the doorway of the patient's room and produced it from the wire basket on the wall, handing it to him.

He scowled. "This nausea started on the last shift. Why wasn't something done about it then?" he demanded.

"Some of the nurses are working twelve hour shifts," she reminded him. "And there were four new cases added to the ward this afternoon, all critical."

"That's no excuse."

"Yes, sir," she said automatically, handing him a pen. "Could you do something about it now?"

He scribbled new orders, and then went in to check the man, who was pale from his ordeal.

He came out scowling. "The catheter was taken out last night and put back in this morning. Why?"

"He didn't void for eight hours. It's standard procedure…"

He stared her down. "He's been throwing up and not drinking very many fluids. The longer that catheter stays in, the more risk there is of infection. I want it taken out and left out until and if he complains of discomfort. Is that clear?"

"Yes, sir," she said.

"Who had the catheter taken out?" he asked abruptly.

She only smiled at him.

"Never mind," he said heavily, knowing that torture wouldn't drag a name out of her. His eyes went over her oval face. Her cheeks were red but the rest of her face was pale and rather puffy. He scowled. He'd never noticed that before. It was the sort of look he often found in heart patients.

She put the chart back up. "The technicians are run off their feet on this shift. I wish we had someone staying with him who could give him cracked ice. That would stay down."

"Hasn't he any family?" he asked, touched by her concern.

"A son, in Utah," she replied. "He's on his way here, but he won't arrive until tomorrow."

"Tough."

"Very."

He glanced toward one of the patient's wives who was trotting down the hall with a foam cup and a plastic pitcher. "Where's she going?" he asked.

Noreen actually smiled, her eyes lighting up. "The Jamaican technician, Mrs. Hawk, told her where the ice machine and the coffee machine were. She's been saving everyone steps ever since. She even gets towels and washcloths and blankets when she needs them, instead of asking anyone."

"This is unusual?"

"Well, there are three other women who come to the door and ask us to give their husbands water when they're thirsty—about every five minutes, after they're brought in here after surgery."

"Nurses used to do those things," he reminded her.

"Nurses used to have more time, fewer patients, less paperwork and not as many lawsuits to worry about," she returned, and sighed.

He searched her face and the frown came back. "Do you feel all right?" he asked with evident reluctance.

Her face closed up. "I'm a little tired, like everyone else on this shift. Thank you for seeing about Mr. Harris, sir."

He shrugged. "Let me know if he has any further bouts of nausea."

"Yes, sir." She was polite, but cool, remote.

His dark eyes narrowed as they met her gray ones. "You don't like me at all, do you?" he asked bluntly, as if he'd only just realized it.

She laughed without humor. "Isn't that my line?"

She turned without meeting his gaze and went back to work, apparently dismissing him from her mind.

He left the ward, but something was nagging at the back of his mind, something he couldn't quite put his finger on. He was uneasy, and he didn't know why.

Vacations, he thought, were supposed to relax people. His seemed to have had an opposite effect.

Behind him, Noreen was trying to calm her renegade heartbeat, forcing herself not to look after the tall, dark man to whom she'd secretly given her heart so long ago. He'd never known, and he never would. Isadora had brought the tall man home and Noreen's heart had broken in two. Not for her, the dark warm eyes, the sensuous smiles. Isadora, the pretty one, the flirting one, married the man Noreen would have died just to kiss. She'd kept her painful secret for six long years, through the four years of Ramon's marriage, through the past two searing years of accusation and persecution. Her heart should have worn out by now, but it kept beating, despite its imperfection that grew worse daily.

The time would come when she might not have time to get to a doctor. Not that it mattered. Her life was one of sacrifice and duty. There had been no love in it since the death of her parents. She'd felt lost going to the big, lonely house that accepted her only reluctantly. She'd been Isadora's private servant, her aunt's social secretary, her uncle's go-for. She'd been alone and lonely most of her adult life, hopelessly in love with her cousin's husband and too proud to ever let it show.

He hated her now, blamed her for something that wasn't really her fault. Even in death, he still belonged to beautiful Isadora. Noreen turned her mind back to her chores, shutting him out, shutting out the past and the pain. She accepted her lot, as she always had, and went about her work.

Two

Noreen went home to her lonely apartment and wished, not for the first time, that she had a cat or a dog or something to keep her company. But the apartment house had strict rules about pets. None were allowed, period. It was a lovely old Southern home, two story, with antiquated plumbing and peeling paint on the walls. But its four residents considered it home, and it boasted a small garage maintained just behind it for the residents who drove.

Fortunately Noreen and a medical student seemed to be the only people in residence who owned cars. There was a Marta bus stop on the corner, and here in midtown, everything was accessible. Noreen, however, liked the freedom her car gave her. It was small and old, but it managed to keep going, thanks to the mechanic down the block who charged only a tiny fee to tinker with it when necessary. While she made a good salary at the hospital, Noreen still had to cut corners to make ends meet.

She'd never lacked for material things when she lived with her aunt and uncle and Isadora, but her life had been emotionally empty. Here, with her few possessions around her, she was at least independent. And if she lacked for love and companionship, that was nothing new. She wondered occasionally if her aunt had minded having to hire a housekeeper and social secretary after Noreen's expulsion from the family home. She'd never had to pay her niece for these services. It would never have occurred to her.

Ramon had moved to a new apartment, she recalled, after Isadora's tragic death. He hadn't been able to face going home to the scene of his beloved wife's last hours, for which he still blamed Noreen. She'd tried and tried to make him listen to the truth, just after it happened. But, maddened with grief and pain, he'd refused to let her speak. Perhaps he preferred the heartless image he'd endowed her with since their first meeting. God knew, he'd never really looked at her anyway.

She recalled with pain her first sight of him, getting out of a stately Jaguar in front of her aunt and uncle's huge, sprawling mansion. His black hair had shone in the sun. His tall, athletic form in a staid gray suit had made him seem leaner, more imposing. As he entered the house, the impact of his liquid, coal black eyes in a handsome, blemishless dark face had caused Noreen's heart to stop dead for an instant. She'd never known such sensations in her life. She'd flushed and stammered, and Ramon had smiled almost mockingly at her momentary weakness. It had been, she recalled painfully, as if he knew that her knees had gone weak in that instant. He was worldly, so perhaps her reaction was one to which he'd become accustomed. But God knew, amusement had been his only expression. He'd turned right away from Noreen after the quick, indifferent introduction, right back to his beautiful Isadora.

"Don't think that he noticed you at all," Isadora had said mockingly that evening, "despite the calf's eyes you were making at him. Imagine a man like that looking twice at you!" she'd added, laughing.

Noreen hadn't been able to meet those demeaning blue eyes. "I know he belongs to you, Isadora," she'd said quietly, tidying up after her cousin.

"Just remember it," came the curt reply. "I'm going to marry him."

"Does he know?" Noreen couldn't resist asking the dry question.

"Of course not," her cousin murmured absently. "But I'm going to, just the same."

And she had, only two months later, with her aunt as matron of honor and one of her set as bridesmaid.

Ramon, courteous to a fault even to strangers, had puzzled over the selection. Two days before the wedding, while Isadora enthused over her bridal gown with her mother, Ramon had paused in the doorway of the kitchen, where Noreen was taking tiny teacakes out of the oven, to ask why she wasn't participating in the wedding.

"Me?" Noreen had asked, sweating from the heat of the kitchen, where she'd been sent to make pastries for afternoon coffee.

He'd frowned at her appearance. "Do you never wear anything except jeans and those—" he waved an expressive dark hand "—sweatshirts?"

She'd averted her eyes. "They're comfortable for working around the house," she'd replied.

She could feel him watching her while she slid the cakes onto a china plate and placed the cookie sheet into the stainless-steel sink for washing.

"Isadora doesn't like to cook," he murmured.

"I imagine you won't mind having someone else do it," she replied uncomfortably. She hated having him even this close, she was so afraid of giving herself away. "Anyway, Isadora's much too pretty to waste time on domestic chores."

"Are you jealous of her," he'd asked, "because she's pretty and you aren't?"

The mocking tone of the question had brought her pale gray eyes up flashing. She almost never talked back, but he seemed to bring out latent temper in her that she hadn't realized she possessed.

She remembered standing up straight, glaring at him from a face flushed with heat and temper, her dark blond hair hanging in limp ringlets from the bun atop her head. "Thank you so much for reminding me of the qualities I lack. I don't suppose it would occur to you that I'm capable of looking in a mirror?"

His eyes had sparkled, for the first time, at her. His eyelids had come down over that glitter and he'd stared at her until her unruly heart had gone crazy in her chest.

"So you're not quite a doormat, then?" he'd prompted.

"No, no soy," she replied in the perfect Spanish she'd been taught in school, *"y usted, señor, no es ningún cabellero."*

His eyebrows had gone up with her assertion that he was no gentleman. *"Que sorpresa eres,"* he murmured, making her flush again with the intimacy of the familiar tense—only used between close friends or relatives—when she'd used the formal. *What a surprise you are!* he'd said.

"Why, because I can speak Spanish?" she asked in English.

He smiled, for once without sarcasm. "Isadora can't. Not yet, at least. I intend to teach her the most necessary words. Of course, those aren't used in public."

From a distance of years, she looked back with faint curiosity at the way he'd taunted her with his feelings for Isadora. It had been that way from the beginning. It grew much worse as the couple celebrated their first anniversary.

Noreen hadn't ever been sure why she was invited to the party. She hadn't planned to go, either, but Ramon had sent a car for her.

Hal and Mary Kensington welcomed her enthusiastically in front of their guests, and then ignored her. Isadora seemed furious to see her there and had pulled her to one side during Ramon's brief absence, with curling fingers whose nails had almost broken the surface of her skin.

"What are you doing here?" she'd demanded furiously. "I didn't invite you to my anniversary celebration!"

"Ramon insisted," Noreen said through her teeth. "He sent a car."

The other woman's delicate blond brows arched. "I see," she murmured. She dropped her cousin's arm abruptly. "He's getting even," she added with a harsh laugh. "Just because I had Larry over to dinner while he was away operating in New York.'' She shifted abruptly. ''Well, he's never home, what does he expect me to do, sit on my hands?'' Her eyes ran over Noreen angrily. ''Don't imagine that he sees stars when he looks at you, sweetie,'' she continued hotly. ''He only made you come so that he could make me jealous.''

Noreen had caught her breath. ''But, that's crazy,'' she'd said, choking. ''For heaven's sake, Isadora, he doesn't even like me! He cuts at me all the time!''

The other woman's deep blue eyes had narrowed. ''You don't understand at all, do you?'' she'd asked absently. ''You're such a child, Norie.''

''Understand what?''

Ramon had come into the kitchen then, his face hard. ''Why are you hiding in here?'' he asked Isadora. ''We have guests.''

''Yes, don't we?'' she replied with a pointed look at Noreen. ''I should have asked Larry,'' she added.

Ramon's eyes had flashed furiously. Isadora darted under his arm and back to her guests, leaving Ramon with only Noreen to take his burst of temper out on.

And he had.

''The charlady, in person,'' he'd commented coldly, glaring at her eternal jeans and sweatshirt. ''You couldn't wear a dress for the occasion?''

''I didn't want to come,'' she replied furiously. ''You made me!''

''God knows why,'' he returned with another cold survey of her person.

She couldn't think of anything to say to him. She felt and looked out of place.

He'd moved closer and she'd backed away. The

expression on his face had been priceless. Sadly, her instinctive action had led to something even worse.

"Do I repulse you?" he'd murmured, coming closer until she was backed to the sink. "Amazing, that such a shadow of a woman would refuse any semblance of ardent notice on the part of a man, even a repulsive man."

She'd shivered at his tone and crossed her arms across her sweatshirt defensively. "A married man." She'd hurled the words at him.

His hands had clenched by his side, although the words had the desired effect. He made no more movements toward her. His eyes had searched hers, demanding answers she couldn't give.

"Maid of all work," he'd taunted, "cook and housekeeper and doer of small tasks. Don't you ever get tired of sainthood?"

She'd swallowed. "I'd like to go now, please."

His chest had risen sharply. "Where would you like to go? Away from me?"

"You're married to my cousin," she'd said through her teeth, fighting down an attraction that made her sick all over.

"Of course I am, house sparrow," he'd replied. "That beautiful, charming woman with the saintly face and body is all mine. Other men are sick with jealousy of what I have. Isadora, bright and beautiful, with my ring on her finger."

"Yes, she is...lovely." She'd choked.

His fury had been a little intimidating. Those black eyes were like swords, cutting at her. He hated her, and she knew it. Only she didn't know why. She'd never hurt him.

He'd moved aside then, with that innate courtesy and formality that was part of him.

"I grew up in a barrio in Havana," he murmured quietly. "My parents struggled to get through college, to educate themselves enough to get out of the poverty. When we came to the States, we rose in position and wealth, but I haven't forgotten my beginnings. Part of me has nothing but contempt for those people in there—" he jerked his head toward the living room "—content in their pure country club environment, ignorant of the ways poverty can twist a soul."

"Why are you talking to me like this?" she'd asked.

His face had softened, just a little. "Because you've known poverty," he replied, surprising her. She hadn't realized he knew anything about her. "Your parents were farmers, weren't they?"

She nodded. "They didn't get along very well with Aunt Mary and Uncle Hal," she confided. "Except for public opinion, I'd have gone to an orphanage when they were killed."

He knew what she meant. "And would an orphanage have been so much worse?"

The question had taunted her, then and now. It was as if he knew what her life had been like with the Kensingtons, her father's brother and sister-in-law, and beautiful Isadora. Ridiculous, of course, to think that he understood.

On the other hand, she wondered if Isadora had ever understood him, or how his childhood had shaped him into the adult he was now. He never refused an indigent patient, or turned his back on anyone who needed help. He was the most generous man she'd ever know.

Isadora hated that facet of his personality.

"He gives money away to people on the street, can you believe it?" Isadora had asked at Christmas the second year of her marriage. "We had an unholy row about it. They're the flotsam of the earth. You don't give money to people like that!"

Noreen didn't say a word. She frequently contributed what little she could spare to a food fund for the homeless, even volunteering during holidays to help serve it.

One day during the holidays, to her amazement, she'd found Ramon putting on an apron over his suit to join her at the serving line.

"Don't look so shocked," he'd said at her expression. "Half the staff sneaks down here at one time or another to do what they can."

She'd ladled soup at his side for an hour in the crowded confines, sick with gratitude for her own meager income and a roof over her head as the hopeless poor of the city crowded into the warmth of the hall for a hot meal. Tears had stung her eyes as a woman with two small children had smiled and thanked them for their one meal of the day.

Ramon's hand had come up into hers with a handkerchief. *"No ¡hagas!"* he'd whispered in Spanish. *Don't do that.*

"I don't imagine you ever shed tears," she'd muttered as she wiped her eyes unobtrusively with the spotless white handkerchief that smelled of exotic spices.

He'd laughed softly. "No?"

She glanced at him curiously.

"I care about my patients," he told her quietly. "I'm not made of stone, when I lose one."

She averted her eyes to the soup and concentrated on putting it into the bowls. "Latins are passionate about everything, they say," she'd murmured without thinking.

"About everything," he'd replied in a tone that made her shiver inexplicably.

She'd tried to give him back the handkerchief, but he'd refused it at first.

His eyes had been cruel as they met hers over it. "Put it under your pillow," he'd chided. "Perhaps the dreams it inspires will make up for the emptiness in your life."

Her gasp of shock had seemed to bring him to his senses.

"I beg your pardon," he'd replied stiffly. And, taking the handkerchief back, he'd shoved it into his slacks pocket as if the sight of it angered him.

Over the years there had been other incidents. Once she'd been summoned by Isadora to drive her downtown when Ramon had refused to let her use the Jaguar.

She'd barely been admitted by the flustered maid when she heard the furious voices coming from the living room.

"I'll spend what I like!" Isadora was yelling at her husband. "God knows, I deserve a few luxuries, since I don't have a husband! You spend every waking hour at the office or in the hospital! We never have meals together! We don't even sleep together…!"

"Isadora!" Noreen had called, to alert her cousin to her appearance before the argument got any hotter.

"What's she doing here?" Noreen heard Ramon

ask furiously as she walked toward the living room, hesitating for a second at the open door.

"She's driving me to the mall," Isadora had told him hatefully, "since you won't!" She glanced toward Noreen. "Well, come in, come in," she called angrily. "Don't stand out there like a shadow!"

Ramon's hot glance told her what he thought of her and her usual, off-duty attire. She was the soul of neatness on the job, in her ward, but she still dressed like a farm girl when she was off duty.

"Honestly, Norie, haven't you got any other clothes?" Isadora asked angrily.

"I don't need any others," she replied, refusing to supply her relative with the information that her salary barely covered her apartment rent and gas for the car, much less fancy clothes.

"How economical you are," Ramon purred.

Isadora had glared at him, jerking up her purse and cashmere sweater. "You should have married her!" She threw the words at him. "She can cook and clean and she dresses like a street person! She probably even likes children!"

Noreen had colored, remembering being with Ramon in the soup kitchen downtown at Christmas.

"How would you know how street people dress?" Ramon asked his wife coolly. "You won't even look at them."

"God forbid," she shuddered. "They should round them all up and put them in jail!"

Noreen, remembering the woman and two little children who'd accepted their meal with such gratitude, felt sick to her stomach and turned away, biting her tongue to keep it silent.

"Spend what the hell you like," Ramon told his wife.

Isadora's eyebrows had risen an inch. "Such language!" she'd chided. "You never used to curse at all."

"I never used to have reason to."

Isadora made a sound in her throat and stalked out, motioning curtly to Noreen to follow her.

Just a week before Isadora died, she was taken with a mild bronchitis. Ramon had promised to accompany a fellow surgeon to Paris for an important international conference on new techniques in open-heart surgery. Isadora had pleaded to go, and Ramon had refused, reminding her that flying in a pressurized cabin on an airplane could be very dangerous for someone with even a mild lung infection.

Typically Isadora had pouted and fumed, but Ramon hadn't listened. He'd stopped by Noreen's station in the cardiac unit at O'Keefe's and asked her to stay with Isadora in their apartment and take care of her in his absence.

"She'll find a way to get even, if she can," he'd said, curiously grim. "Watch her like a hawk. Promise me you won't leave her if she takes a turn for the worse."

"I promise," she'd said.

"And get her to a hospital if there's any deterioration at all. She has damaged lungs from all that smoking she used to do, and she's very nearly asthmatic," he'd added. "Pneumonia could be fatal."

"I'll look after her," she'd said again.

His dark eyes had searched hers relentlessly. "You're nothing like her," he'd said quietly.

Her face had gone taut. "Thanks for reminding me. Are there any other insults you'd like to add, before you go?"

He'd looked shocked. "It wasn't meant as an insult."

"Of course not," she'd replied dryly. She'd turned back to her work. "I know you can't stand the sight of me, Ramon, but I do care about my cousin, whether you believe it or not. I'll take good care of her."

"You're an excellent nurse."

"No need to butter me up," she said wearily, having grown used to the technique over the years. "I've already said I'll stay with her."

His hand, surprisingly, had caught her arm and jerked her around. His eyes were blazing.

"I don't use flattery to get what I want," he said curtly. "Least of all with you."

"All right," she'd agreed, trying to loosen his painful grip.

He seemed not to realize how tight he was holding her arm. He even shook it, having totally lost his self-control for the first time in recent memory. "Make her understand why she can't go on the plane. She won't listen to me."

"I will. But you should be pleased that she wants your company so much."

His grip tightened. "One of the men who will be at the conference is her lover," he said with a short laugh. "That's why she's so eager to go."

Noreen's face was a study in shock.

"You didn't know?" he asked very softly. "I can't satisfy her," he added bluntly. "No matter how long I take, whatever I do. She needs more than one man

a night, and I'm worn to the bone when I get home
from the hospital.''

"Please," she'd whispered, embarrassed, "you
shouldn't be telling me this...!''

"Why not?" he'd asked irritably. "Who else can
I tell? I have no close friends, my parents are dead, I
have no siblings. There isn't a human being on earth
who's ever managed to get close to me, until now."
He searched her face with eyes that hated it. "Damn
you, Noreen," he whispered fervently. "Damn you!"

He dropped her arm and stalked off the ward, leaving her shaken and white with shock. He really hated
her. That was when the mask had come down and
she'd seen it in his eyes, in his face. She didn't know
why he hated her. Perhaps because Isadora had said
something to him...

She'd gone to their apartment that night, confident
that Ramon had already left, to find the maid hysterical and Isadora sitting out on the balcony in a filmy
nightgown, in the icy cold February rain.

She'd been out there, the poor maid cried, ever
since her husband had left the apartment. She didn't
know what had been said between them, but she'd
heard the voices, loud and unsettling, in their bedroom. There had been a furious argument, and just
after the doctor had gone, the madam had taken off
her robe and gone to sit in the rain. Nothing would
induce her to come inside. She was coughing furiously already and she had a high fever that she'd
forbidden the maid to tell the doctor about.

Noreen had gone at once to the balcony and with
the maid's help, had dragged Isadora back inside.

They'd changed her clothing, but the effort had made Noreen's heart, always frail, beat erratically.

While she was catching her breath, the maid announced that her husband had already phoned twice and was furious. She had to leave.

Noreen was reluctant to let her go, feeling sick already, but the poor girl was in tears. She gave permission for her to leave, and then went to listen to Isadora's chest.

Her cousin was breathing strangely. She wasn't conscious, and her fever was furiously high.

She had to get an ambulance, she decided, and went to phone for one. But when she lifted the receiver, there was a strange sound and no dial tone.

Furious, she started out into the hall to ask a neighbor to phone for her. Suddenly everything went pitchblack.

She was really frightened now, and her heart was acting crazily.

She moved down the hall, feeling for the elevators, but they weren't working. There was the staircase. They were only four flights up. It wouldn't be too far. She had a terrible feeling that Isadora's lung had collapsed. She could die...

Making a terrific effort, she pushed into the stairwell and started down and down, holding on to the rail for support as her breathing began to change and her heartbeat hurt.

She never really remembered afterward what happened, except that she suddenly lost her footing, and consciousness, at the same time.

She came to in the hospital, trying to explain to a white-coated stranger that she must get back to her cousin. But the man only patted her arm and gave her an injection.

It was the next day before she was able to get out of the hospital and go back to Ramon's apartment. But by that time, the maid had found Isadora dead, and worst of all, Ramon had come home before she was moved.

Noreen had arrived at the door just as the ambulance attendants came out with Isadora's body.

Ramon had seen Noreen and lapsed into gutter Spanish that questioned everything from Noreen's parentage to her immediate future, eloquently.

"Oh, please, let me explain!" she'd pleaded, in tears as she realized what must have happened to Isadora, poor Isadora, all alone and desperately ill. "Please, it wasn't my fault! Let me tell you...!"

"Get out of my apartment!" Ramon had raged, in English now that he'd exhausted himself of insults. "I'll hate you until I die for this, Noreen. I'll never forgive you as long as I live! You let her die!"

She'd stood there, numb with shock and weakness, as he strode out behind the ambulance, his face white and drawn.

Later, at the funeral home, Noreen had tried to talk to her aunt and uncle, but her aunt had slapped her and her uncle had refused to even look at her. Ramon had demanded that she be removed from the premises and not allowed to return.

She hadn't been allowed at the service, either. She was an outcast from that moment until just recently, when inexplicably, her aunt and uncle had invited her for coffee just before her uncle's birthday. Ramon's attitude had been one of unyielding hatred.

Her feelings of guilt were only magnified by the attitude of Isadora's husband and parents. Eventually she realized that nothing was going to excuse her part in what had happened, and she'd accepted her guilt as if she deserved it. Her work had become her life. She never asked for anything from her relatives again. Not even for forgiveness.

Three

It had been a long morning and Ramon was worn to the bone. He'd already done one meticulous bypass operation and a valve was scheduled first thing after lunch. It should have been his day off, but he was covering at O'Keefe for one of the other surgeons who was sick with a bad case of the flu.

He carried his tray into the cafeteria dining room and looked around the crowded area, hoping for an empty table, but there wasn't one. The only empty spot he glimpsed was at a table occupied by Noreen. He glared at her over his salad plate and coffee.

Noreen dropped her eyes back to her plate, furious with herself for flushing when he looked at her. He'd take his salad out to the small canteen adjoining the cafeteria and sit on the floor before he'd join her, and she knew it. If only she could outrun her own hated feelings for the horrible man. If only it didn't matter what he thought of her.

She almost dropped her fork when, without asking, he put his coffee and plate down on the table across from her, pulled out a chair and sat down.

He saw her surprise and was almost amused by it. He spread his napkin in his lap, took the plastic lid from his salad plate and picked up his own fork.

"Would sitting on the floor have been too obvious?" she asked in a faintly dry tone.

His dark gaze pinned hers for an instant before he bent his head toward a forkful of tuna salad.

"You do that so well," she remarked.

"Do what?" he asked.

She finished a mouthful of fruit and sat back in her chair. "Snub me," she said. "I suppose I irritated you from the day we met, just by being alive."

"Don't talk nonsense," he murmured deeply, and sipped his coffee. He glanced at the clock. "I thought you went to lunch at half-past noon."

She crossed her long legs in their white knit slacks. "I usually do. But you weren't supposed to be operating at O'Keefe today," she explained.

His black eyes twinkled a little. "You avoid me, then?"

"Of course I avoid you," she replied tersely. "That's what you want me to do. You don't even have to say it." She stared into her black coffee, idly noting that he took his coffee black, too.

His gaze ran over her averted profile. She wasn't pretty, as Isadora had been. But she was slender and had a nice shape, even though her features were ordinary. Her hair was neither blond nor light brown, but somewhere in between. Her eyes were more gray than blue. She never wore makeup. In fact, she seemed not to care how she looked, although she was always clean and neat in appearance. She might be quite attractive with the right hairstyle and clothes. His eyes narrowed on the thick bun at her nape. He'd never seen her with her hair down. He'd wondered for a long time what it would look like, loosened.

She caught his speculative glance and her cheeks colored. "I feel like a moth on a pin," she murmured. "Could you stop staring at me? I know you think I'm the nearest thing to an ax-murderess, but you don't have to make it so obvious in public, do you?"

He scowled. "I haven't said a word."

She laughed, but it had a hollow sound. Her gray eyes were full of disillusionment and loneliness. "No," she agreed. "You never have. You may be Latin, but you don't act it anymore. You never explode in rage, or throw things, or curse at the top of your lungs. You can get further with a look than most doctors can with arm-waving fury. You don't have to say anything. Your eyes say it for you."

His dark eyes narrowed. "And what are they telling you?"

"That you blame me for Isadora," she said quietly. "That you hate me. That you wake up every morning wishing it had been me instead of her in that casket."

His jaw clenched, to keep the words back. His eyes glittered, just the same.

"You might not believe it," she added heavily, "but there are times when I wish I could have taken her place. None of you seemed to realize that I loved her, too. I grew up with Isadora. She could be cruel, but she could be kind when she liked. I miss her."

He tried unsuccessfully to bite back the cold words.

"What an odd way you had of showing your concern," he muttered curtly. "Leaving her alone in an apartment to die." The minute the words were out, he regretted them deeply, but it was already too late.

Noreen's eyes closed. She felt faint, as she did so often these days. Her breath came in short little shallow breaths. She clenched her hands in her lap and fought to stay calm, so that she wouldn't betray herself. Ramon was an excellent surgeon. She wouldn't be able to hide her condition if he looked too closely. He might say something to administration...

She lifted her head seconds later, pale but more stable. "I have to go," she said, and slowly, carefully, got out of her chair, holding on to it for support.

"Have you had any sleep?" he asked suddenly.

"You mean, does my guilty conscience keep me awake?" she said for him, smiling coolly. "Yes, if you want to know, it does. I would have saved Isadora if I'd been able to."

She was fine-drawn, as if she didn't eat or sleep. "You never told me exactly what happened," he said.

The statement surprised her. "I tried to," she reminded him. "I tried to tell all of you. But nobody wanted my side of the story."

"Maybe I want it now," he replied.

"Two years too late," she told him. She picked up her tray. "I would gladly have told you then. But I won't bother now. It doesn't matter anymore." Her eyes were empty of all feeling as her gaze met his, betraying nothing of the turmoil he kindled inside her. "It doesn't matter at all what any of you think of me."

She turned away and went slowly to the automatic

tray return to deposit her dishes. She didn't look back as she went out the door toward the staff elevators.

Ramon's dark eyes followed her with bitter regret. He couldn't seem to stop hurting her. It was the last thing she needed. She moved more slowly these days. She didn't seem to have an interest in anything beyond her work. The hospital grapevine was fairly dependable about romances and breakups, but he'd never heard Noreen's name coupled with that of any of the hospital staff. She didn't date. Even when she was living at home with Isadora's family, she was forever walking around with her nose stuck in a medical book, studying for tests and final exams. She'd graduated nurses' training with highest honors, he recalled, and no wonder.

He sipped his coffee, remembering his first glimpse of her. He'd met Isadora at a charity dinner, and they'd had an instant rapport. Isadora's date had been appropriated by his boss for a late sales meeting, and Ramon had offered to drive the beautiful blonde home. She'd accepted at once.

She lived in a huge Georgian mansion on the outskirts of Atlanta, in a fashionable neighborhood. Her parents had been in the living room watching the late news when she'd introduced Ramon to them. They were standoffish at first, until Isadora told them what he did for a living and how famous he was becoming.

Noreen had been at home. She was curled up in a big armchair by the fireplace with an anatomy book in her hands, a pair of big-rimmed reading glasses perched on her nose. He remembered even now the look in her eyes when he and Isadora had approached her. Those soft gray eyes had kindled with a kind of gentle fire, huge and luminous and full of warm secrets. He'd made an instant impression on her; he saw it in her radiant face, felt it in the slight tremor of her small hand when they were introduced. But he had eyes only for Isadora, and it was apparent. Noreen had withdrawn with an odd little smile.

And in the weeks that followed, while he courted Isadora, Noreen was conspicuous by her absence. She hadn't been invited to be part of the wedding. Later, it shamed him to remember how insulting Isadora had been about her cousin. She hadn't wanted to include Noreen among her entourage. Isadora had been viciously jealous of her cousin. She seemed to delight in looking for ways to put Noreen down, to make her feel unwelcome or inferior.

Isadora had been beautiful, socially acceptable, poised and talented. But she was empty inside, as Noreen wasn't. That jealousy had led to a bitter argument before Ramon's trip to Paris just before Isadora's death. He closed his eyes and shuddered inside, remembering what had been said. He'd blamed Noreen for everything, even for that, when the blame was equally his.

The movement of people at the next table brought him back from his musings. He glanced at his watch and hurriedly finished his lunch. It was time to go back to work.

Noreen was anxious to get back to her apartment after she finished her day's work. She was feeling weaker by the minute, breathless and faintly nauseous, and her heartbeat was so irregular that it bothered her.

She got into bed and laid down. She was asleep

before she realized it, too tired to even bother with so much as a bowl of cereal for supper.

But by morning, she felt better and her pulse seemed less erratic. She had to continue working. If she lost her job, she could lose her medical insurance, and she had to depend on it for the valve surgery she needed. It was an expensive operation, but without it she might not live a great deal longer. She knew that the damaged valve was leaking, the specialist had told her so. But she also knew that people could live a long time with a leaky valve, depending on the amount of leakage there was and the level of medical care and supervision she had. Until now, she'd had very few problems since Isadora's death.

She sipped orange juice and grimaced as she recalled how sick Isadora had been and how desperate she'd been to get help. Ramon wanted to know all about it now, and that was tragic, because she wasn't going to tell him a thing. She had no place in his life at all, nor did she want one. She'd paid too high a price for her feelings already. She wasn't going to fall back into the trap of loving him. Loneliness was safer.

Sometimes Noreen wondered about the argument with Ramon that had sent her cousin out into the cold rain with pneumonia. She'd had antibiotics for the bronchitis, which she insisted that she could give herself, without Noreen's help. Later, Noreen had discovered the full bottle of antibiotic tucked between the mattress and box springs.

Isadora had been furious with Ramon for not taking her with him to France. Or at least, that was what she said. But the maid had alluded to a furious argument before he left, and that had never been mentioned again. At least, not to Noreen. Ramon had said something about Isadora punishing him for not letting her go along. There had been the mention of a lover, as well. Despite Isadora's attempt to portray her marriage as perfection itself, Noreen had known better.

Odd how Ramon tried to idolize the marriage, now that Isadora was gone.

Noreen wondered if Isadora had really meant to die, or if she'd just miscalculated about the dangers of any such drastic exposure with pneumonia, and she'd died because of it. Perhaps it hadn't occurred to her that damaged lungs could collapse and become fatal. Despite living with a surgeon for four years, she hadn't seemed to know much at all about medicine or illness.

Ramon didn't know that Isadora had deliberately exposed herself to the rain and cold. The maid, after finding Isadora's body, had collapsed in hysteria and never came back, even to get her check. Noreen hadn't seen her again. So Ramon only knew that Noreen had left Isadora alone, and Isadora had died. Neither he nor Isadora's parents would let Noreen tell her side of the story. They grieved and cursed her and even two years after the fact, they all still blamed her.

It wasn't as if they loved her, of course, or as if they cared about her own grief for her beautiful, selfish cousin. Despite their spats, Isadora and Noreen had grown up together, and they felt some sort of affection for each other. But the Kensingtons locked Noreen out of their lives. It had come as a gigantic surprise when her aunt had invited her over for coffee and cake the week of her uncle's birthday. The conversation had been stilted, and Noreen hadn't enjoyed it. She supposed that people were talking about their avoidance of Noreen and their refusal to forgive her.

She couldn't think of any other reason they'd have wanted her company. Her aunt did hate gossip.

She went to work and managed to get through her shift without much difficulty, but the amount of breathlessness she was having disturbed her.

That afternoon, she got an appointment with a colleague of her Macon surgeon, and was worked in at the end of the day.

He had tests run, and he listened to her heart. He was a tall, fair man with an easy smile and a nice disposition.

"You're a nurse," he reminded her. "Can't you tell when a heart isn't working properly?"

"Yes. But I hoped it was just overwork."

"It is," he said. "And that valve is leaking a little more than it was. You need to schedule the surgery, and it should be soon. I don't want to alarm you, but if that valve goes all at once, there may not even be time to get you to a hospital. Surely you know that?"

She did. How could she tell him that at times she thought it might be a relief not to have to face another day of Ramon's cold antagonism and accusation?

I'm dying of unrequited love, she thought to herself and laughed out loud at the whimsical thought. *I have a broken heart, in more ways than one.*

"It isn't cause for levity," the doctor said firmly, misunderstanding her chuckle. "I want to talk to Dr. Myers, the surgeon, and get you scheduled for surgery." His eyes narrowed. "Your late cousin was married to Dr. Ramon Cortero. He's the very best heart surgeon around. He trained at Johns Hopkins. Why can't he do the surgery?"

"He doesn't know there's anything wrong with me, and I don't want him to know," she said flatly.

"But why not?"

"Because he hates me. He might let something slip about my condition and I could lose my job," she told him. "I can't afford to let that happen. My medical insurance is critical right now. I don't dare let them know that I'm having such terrible problems with my health."

"They wouldn't fire you," he said.

"They might," she snapped back. "I wouldn't blame them. A nurse should be in the peak of health when she's responsible for patients in an intensive care unit. I'm keenly aware of my limitations. That's why I insisted that they have another RN on duty with me, just in case." She smiled faintly. "I didn't tell them why, of course."

He shook his head. "You're playing a dangerous game. You could die."

She got up from her chair. "We all do, eventually."

He got up, too, scowling. "Don't wait too long," he pleaded. "They love you at O'Keefe. I have patients there, so I hear all the gossip." He studied her wan face. "You never told Cortero why you weren't with his wife when she died. Why not?"

"Because he wouldn't listen," she replied. "And now, it doesn't matter." She pushed back a loose wisp of blond hair. "It's easier for me if he goes on hating me. Please don't ask why."

"I won't. But promise me you'll do something soon."

"I will," she agreed. She drew in a long breath. "It's just thinking about the length of time I'll lose from work. I don't know how I'll survive."

"There are all sorts of agencies that can help. Your

aunt and uncle endowed a whole pediatric wing at St. Mary's. Surely they'd help you.''

She laughed. ''They hate me even more than Ramon does,'' she told him. She shrugged. ''It's just as well. If I die on the operating table, nobody's going to grieve for me. Nobody in the world.''

She thanked him for his time and went out, clutching the prescriptions she'd persuaded him to give her, to stabilize her heartbeat and thin her blood, and buy her just a little more time before she had the surgery. In another three weeks, she'd have enough saved to pay her rent for two months in advance. If her insurance paid eighty percent of the hospital bill, which it was supposed to, she could almost manage financially.

''You look like death warmed over,'' Brad Donaldson muttered as she came onto the ward. Brad was a technician, and a good one. He'd started at O'Keefe about the same time Noreen had, four years ago. He was the only real friend she had, although it was just the friendship of colleagues. Brad was eating his heart out over a young lady doctor who was working as a resident in the emergency room. She couldn't see him for dust. It made for fellow feeling that they were both dying of unrequited love, even though Brad didn't know who Noreen was pining for.

''I feel like death warmed over,'' she told him.

He cocked his blond head and watched her closely. ''Your color isn't very good.''

''I know.'' She took a steadying breath. ''I'll be all right. The doctor gave me something to help stabilize my heartbeat.''

''Talk to me,'' he said.

She smiled, and shook her head. "No. It's my problem. I'll handle it."

"You worry me," he murmured. "What is it about nurses that they never admit when they're sick?"

"All guts, no brains?" she ventured, and smiled. "Come on. We've got treatments to give and lunch on the way, and doctors about to make rounds. Let's get this show on the road."

"After you," he said with a flourish.

A female valve patient was brought up to the ward an hour before Noreen was due to go off duty. She supervised the porters as they got the woman to bed, and then connected the oxygen and the drip, checking the chart for any other medications that the surgeon had ordered. This was one of Ramon's patients. She knew the signature scrawled on the white form.

The woman's eyes opened. She looked white and sick and frightened.

Noreen put a hand on her forehead and gently stroked her gray hair back from the clammy skin. "You're on the cardiac ward. We're going to take wonderful care of you. I'm Noreen. If you need anything at all, just push this button." She guided the woman's thin fingers to the button on the bed rail. "Okay?"

"Dry," the woman croaked. "So…dry."

"Do you have any family to stay with you?" Noreen asked.

"Nobody," came the wan reply. Her eyes closed on a sigh. "Nobody…in the world."

Noreen's heart ached for the poor soul. That's how she felt, and this was how she was going to be after surgery, too—all alone without even a friend to sit and hold her hand. She was going to have her surgery in Macon, to be sure that Ramon knew nothing about it. So even Brad wouldn't be there to sit with her. It was a sobering thought.

"I'll get you some ice," she promised the woman. "It will help a little. You're due for medication, too. I'll bring that back with me."

"Thank you," the woman whispered hoarsely.

"It's my job," she replied with a gentle smile. "Back in a jiffy."

She went to the ice machine and found one of the other patient's wives there filling a bucket.

"I'm superfluous," she told Noreen with a weary grin. "He can pour his own juice and get his own ice now, so I'm just company in between television programs."

Noreen's eyes twinkled. "I don't suppose you'd like to feed cracked ice to the new patient down the hall from you? She has no family and she's dying of thirst."

"I'd love to" came the reply. "Poor soul. There are so many of us in my family that we had volunteers for every hour of the day, but Saul just wants us to stop bothering him so that he can watch his soap operas." She chuckled. "You don't know what a joy it is to see him sitting up in bed and smiling again. I thought we were going to lose him."

"He's tough. I'm glad he came through. Mrs. Charles would be very grateful for any time you could spare to sit with her."

"I'd love to. It will give me something to do with all my spare time."

They filled ice buckets and Noreen took her in to

introduce her to the elderly woman. They struck up an immediate friendship, as well.

Noreen went back to the circular nurses' station that she shared with the other people on her shift, pausing long enough to sip some coffee while she keyed the vital information about Mrs. Charles into the computer.

Brad paused beside her chair. "Should you be ingesting all that caffeine?" he asked so that only she could hear.

She grimaced. "I didn't think. No, I probably shouldn't."

"You need looking after, honey child," he teased, and laid a big hand on her shoulder as he smiled down at her.

Ramon, coming onto the ward, saw the way Brad was leaning over Noreen, saw the smile and the familiarity of that hand on her shoulder. Fury shot through him.

He stopped in front of the nurses' station and glared at Noreen, who noticed him belatedly and stopped smiling at once.

"I want to see Mrs. Charles," he said without preamble. "If you can spare the time?" he added with a cold glance at Brad, who actually blushed.

"She's in here," Noreen said, leading the way to Mrs. Charles's room without looking at her companion. That comment had been unfair and unkind. She worked as hard as he did. Brad was only being nice, but it wouldn't occur to Ramon that anyone wanted to treat her kindly. He thought she was a murderess, someone without feelings of any sort.

She led the way into Mrs. Charles's room. The elderly lady smiled warmly when she saw Ramon.

"Thank you," she said weakly, extending a hand. "You saved...my life."

"My pleasure," he replied, and held the hand. "I've ordered something for pain. Take it when you need it. It won't hurt you. Rest is the very best thing right now. In a day or so, we'll have you up on your feet and get you moving." He frowned. "Do you have any family that we can notify?"

She shook her head. "All dead," she said sadly. "But Mrs. Green feeds me cracked ice. It was this nice young lady's idea."

Ramon glanced at Noreen. "Saving yourself some steps?" he asked in a soft, but accusing, tone.

Noreen ignored the comment and busied herself straightening the sheet over Mrs. Charles's thin body. "If you need us, just call," she said.

"I won't," came the kind reply. "You've all been very good to me."

"It's easy to be kind to someone as nice as you," Noreen replied, smiling.

Ramon checked his patient, murmured with satisfaction and called a cheerful goodbye as he went out of the room and pulled the door closed behind him.

"How dare you put a visitor in charge of nursing my patient?" he demanded with pure fury in his voice the minute they were out of earshot of the patient.

Noreen's heart jumped and ran away with an annoying lack of rhythm. She had to get her breath before she could even answer him. "I didn't," she said. "Mrs. Green's husband is almost ready to go home and he doesn't want her standing over him. She wanted something to do, and I don't have time to feed cracked ice to your patients every five minutes. I know my job. You don't need to tell me how to do it, sir,'' she added deliberately. "Mrs. Green volunteered her time. I didn't ask her to.''

That was quite reasonable, but he was furious about Brad's intimacy with her and even more furious that it should bother him.

"I'll expect my patient's chart to be kept up-to-date constantly. If there's any change in her condition, I want to be notified. I don't care if it's three in the morning.''

"Yes, sir.'' She clutched the chart against her breasts. "She has an arrythmia.''

"She waited almost too long for the surgery,'' he replied. "It was touch and go in the operating room, and it still is. Watch her carefully.''

"I will.'' It was making her nervous to know how crucial timing was to a valve surgery. What if she waited too long? She was younger than Mrs. Charles, but she had an arrythmia of her own…

Ramon noticed the flutter of her flowered cotton jacket, a touch of color that nurses favored over strictly white pants and jacket. He frowned. "Are you all right?'' he asked. "Your heartbeat is…odd.''

It was even odder, thanks to the observation. Her breath was coming too fast. "It's standing so close to you, sir,'' she whispered, her voice dramatic but so low that nobody else could hear. She opened her eyes very wide. "It's so exciting…!'' she said in a theatrical tone.

He muttered something in Spanish that she was glad she couldn't translate, then turned and stalked away down the corridor. She sighed with relief. Well, she'd survived that unexpected bout of curiosity. She wondered why he noticed her heartbeat in the first place. Surely it would suit him if it stopped altogether…

Four

The stress of her deteriorating condition and the pressure of work knocked Noreen flat two days later. She couldn't even lift her head, much less go to work. She called in sick, attributing her illness to a bout of flu, and she promised rashly to be back in two days. That would carry her through her day off, which would be the next day, and give her a little time to get past the weakness. She only hoped that it was overwork and not the valve getting worse.

Brad stopped by after work to bring her some soup and a sandwich from the local deli. She was so weak that she could barely walk to the door, and out of breath when she got back to her bed with Brad a step behind.

"This won't do," he said darkly. "You're going to kill yourself if you don't give in and have the surgery."

"I need...three more weeks to...add to my savings," she explained, white with the exertion and breathlessness. "Then I can pay my rent while...I recuperate."

"You stubborn little idiot," he muttered. "Why doesn't your family realize there's something wrong with you?"

"They never see me. They're only my aunt and uncle. My parents died years ago in an automobile crash."

"They raised you. Don't they care at all?"

"I think they did a little, before Isadora died," she added sadly. "I wish I could change the past. I wish so much that I could. But it's all over."

"Poor little scrap," he said heavily. He patted her hand. "Can you eat something? I brought soup and a sandwich."

"Thank you," she said. "I'll have it tonight, but I don't think I could keep anything down just now."

"Let me call the surgeon."

She shook her head. "Not yet. I'll be better in the morning. I know I will. And I don't have to go back in for two days. Surely, in that length of time..."

"At least stay in bed," Brad pleaded. "Don't exert."

"I won't."

He stayed for a few minutes longer, then he had to go back on duty. She felt more alone than ever when he'd closed and locked the door behind him.

She didn't have the soup. She slept the clock around. And although she did feel better that afternoon, much more able to get around, she was far from recovered. Time was running out.

* * *

It was pouring rain the morning she went back to work. On her way out the door, she heard a pitiful mewing sound, and looked down to find a tiny kitten under one of the hedges that flanked the walkway. It was cold and shivering, and its ribs showed right through the skin.

"Oh, you poor little thing," she cooed, bending to lift it. It purred and purred, rubbing its head against her chin. She looked at it with a rueful smile. The apartment house didn't allow pets. But surely one little kitten...

She stuck it under her coat and went back up the stairs to her apartment, panting for breath when she reached the landing. She put the kitten in the efficiency kitchen with some milk and a little leftover meat loaf. She put a box-top lid down with a newspaper to line it and shut the kitten in the room, hoping for the best. If she got kicked out, perhaps she could find an apartment somewhere else, but she couldn't leave the kitten out in the freezing cold rain.

It would be company, she thought, and a warm glow rose in her chest as she got into her small car and tried to start it. The engine had been acting up, but she couldn't afford a tune-up. She was going to have to make do until after her surgery. But the car refused to start.

She had to sit down and rest enough to catch her breath before she went to wait for the bus. It came, and she got to work.

It was the longest day she could ever remember. She'd told her co-workers that she'd been out with flu, but now two of the nurses on her ward really were out with flu. The nursing staff was shorthanded and as a result, Noreen had to work double shift. The added hours couldn't have come at a worse time.

"This is ridiculous," Brad muttered, watching her prop her back against a wall in the coffee room to catch her breath. "You'll collapse at this rate."

"I have to work," she told him, her eyes as weary as her body. "There wasn't anyone else to call, and I have had two days off, you know."

He studied her wan complexion. "You look worse now than you did at the apartment."

"Thanks. You're gorgeous, too."

He chuckled. "What am I going to do with you?"

"Don't you have something to do?" she murmured.

"A question I was about to ask," came a deep voice from the doorway.

They both turned, to find Ramon Cortero glaring at them with a clipboard chart in his hand. "Do either of you work here? I want to know why my patient hasn't had his 5:00 p.m. dose of blood thinner." He waved the chart at her.

Noreen blinked at him. Her mind was as tired as her body. She blinked. "Which patient?"

"Mr. Hayes," he replied tersely. "It's 8:00 p.m."

"I've been slow," she said miserably. "I'm sorry." She moved away from the wall. "I'll make sure he gets it at once."

"And I'll check the charts of my other three patients while I'm doing rounds," he said angrily. "Just to make certain there were no other…lapses." He followed her, glaring toward Brad.

"It wasn't Brad's fault," she began.

"Oh, I'm aware of that," he replied, his eyes flashing. "Like most men, he's vulnerable to overt flirting."

She closed her teeth together with a snap. "I don't flirt."

"Call it what you like. I'll wait while you get Mr. Hayes's medicine."

She fetched it, still grinding her teeth. He was right, she'd been slow and it could have serious repercussions. If she hadn't been pulling a double shift after two days in bed, it never would have happened.

She gave Mr. Hayes his dose and double-checked all the other files. The vital signs were all neatly charted, but she'd forgotten to measure the urine volume on Mrs. Green. She could have groaned aloud, for all the good it would have done her.

"I won't report this," Ramon told her when he'd finished his rounds. "But make one more mistake, and I'll go straight to the administrator. I won't have my patients put at risk by a nurse's incompetence."

"I'm not incompetent," she began.

"Play with Donaldson on your own time," he added curtly.

"I wasn't…!"

He didn't pause to listen to any more excuses. He stalked off the ward, his lean body rippling with bad temper.

Noreen had to bite back tears. He seemed to hate her more every day she lived. Nothing was going to change his mind about her; she knew that now.

Brad came out of a patient's room, having started the patient on the breathing machine for his inhalant medication.

He glanced around. "Has he gone?" he asked hopefully.

She nodded. She pushed back her hair and shook her head. "I don't know what I'm going to do. I fouled up really good. Someone could have died."

"Not from having one dose of medicine a little late," he said, comforting her. "I should have paid more attention. I'm supposed to be your backup." He put an affectionate arm around her. "Chin up, girl. You'll get through this."

"Heavens, I hope so," she said wearily. She glanced at the clock. "Another hour and I can go home."

"See the surgeon," Brad said solemnly. "You're taking a risk."

Her shoulders slumped. "I suppose I am. Maybe that extra money doesn't matter so much after all. Do you like cats?" she added hopefully.

He shook his head and grinned. "I'm allergic to them. Why?"

"Oh. Never mind." She still had to worry about what to do with the new cat. Perhaps she could work out something with another member of the staff. She'd have to wait and see.

She finished her work, barely, and went off duty after she'd briefed her relief nurse. It was still pouring rain and cold outside. But she heard Ramon's scathing words in her head the whole way, and never noticed the icy wetness on her cheeks.

Ramon came back onto the ward less than half an hour after Noreen had left it, to make one last check of his patients before he went home. He examined carefully the man whose blood thinners had been given later than scheduled and noted that his progress continued. He was vaguely disturbed with himself for

his attack on Noreen. It wasn't like her to be slow
with medicines or overlook notations on the charts.
He wondered what had happened.

Brad was just coming out of his last patient's room
with his equipment when he saw Ramon waiting for
him. He squared his shoulders for a frontal assault,
because the surgeon looked more formidable than
usual with that scowl on his lean face.

"Why was Noreen slow with the medicine?" he
asked bluntly.

Brad's mouth pulled down. "Because she'd been
out-sick for two days and had to work a double shift
tonight. Two of the RNs are down with flu."

Ramon's face tautened. "I see."

Brad searched the taller man's eyes. "You really
should take a good look at Noreen," he replied quietly.

"What do you mean?"

Brad wanted so badly to tell him. But it was Noreen's secret, not his. "Never mind. It's not my business." He nodded and went on his way.

Ramon recorded his notes, and then drove himself
home. But even as he pulled into his garage, he knew
he wouldn't be able to sleep until he'd apologized to
Noreen. With a sigh of resignation, he reversed the
car out of the garage and drove the few miles to the
apartment house where Noreen lived.

She sounded shocked when he rang the buzzer in
her apartment, but she did let him in the front door.
She was waiting at her door when he came up the
flight of stairs. It was a modest apartment house, with
only four occupants, but it was clean and not too spartan.

"What do you want?" Noreen asked, clutching her

blue checked housecoat close at the throat. She was barefoot and disheveled, as if she'd been in bed. Surely not; it was barely nine-thirty.

"Donaldson told me you'd been pulling a double shift," he said shortly. "I didn't know."

Her eyebrows arched. "Would it have mattered? I can't think why. Jumping to conclusions about me seems to be your main form of entertainment."

His brows drew together. "All the same, I don't like berating you for…" He paused as he heard a soft sound in the apartment. "What's that?"

She grimaced, quickly looking up and down the hall and toward the staircase. She pulled her housecoat closer and stepped back. "Please come in."

He stepped into the small combination living and dining room and she quickly shut the door, just as a tiny ball of fur came trundling out of the kitchen mewing.

He gaped at it. The tiny thing was smaller than her foot, barely weaned by the look of it, and half-starved to boot. She bent and picked it up, cuddling it under her chin. It purred and purred.

"I'm not allowed to have pets," she explained. "But I couldn't leave it out in the cold rain. It's so tiny."

That was when he really began to have doubts about Noreen's part in Isadora's death. He couldn't drag his eyes away from the tiny kitten in her arms. She had a soft heart. People were forever imposing on her, because she was a sucker for a sob story. Her aunt used to complain about the number of stray animals Noreen would bring home, which had to be properly treated and then given to good homes. Her aunt and uncle didn't approve of pets, so Noreen was never allowed to have any. But that didn't stop her from rescuing the downtrodden of the animal population.

What bothered him about that memory was what it told him about her. She wouldn't even abandon a stray kitten to its fate, so what in the world ever made him think that she'd sacrifice a cousin whom she loved? It was so out of character that he was amazed at how easily he'd blamed her for Isadora's death.

She noticed the sudden paleness of Ramon's face under his swarthy tan and she clutched the kitten closer.

"What do you want?" she asked with accusing eyes. "I'm very tired and I want to go to sleep."

He studied her through different eyes. Her face was wan and there were bright patches on her cheeks. Her breath was erratic, quick. He could see her heart beating against the fabric of the robe, erratically. Something was wrong here.

"Have you seen a doctor?"

"For a virus?" She laughed, bluffing. "Why would I bother a doctor with something that will wear itself out?"

"I have my bag down in the car," he began.

Her already erratic heart went wild at just the thought of having him listen to her chest. "I have a doctor of my own," she said through her teeth. "And why do you think I'd let you examine me, even if I were dying?" she added bitterly. "I'd never trust you with a scalpel in your hand. The temptation might be too much for you!"

His sharp intake of breath was audible. "How dare you!" he said through his teeth.

She was too sick to be intimidated by that black

glare. "I'm tired," she said, backing up a step. "Would you please go away and let me sleep?"

He hesitated. Something was wrong, and she didn't trust him enough to tell him what it was. He was suddenly less self-assured. He felt guilty, though God knew why he should. He looked at her with open curiosity, seeing the thinness of her, the dark circles under her eyes.

"You're ill," he exclaimed softly, as if just realizing it.

"I'm tired," she repeated. "I got out of bed too soon after a viral infection, and I did too much. I'll be fine tomorrow. I don't need a doctor to tell me that, either."

Her cheekbones were high. She had a lovely mouth, just the right shape and size. Her skin was creamy and faintly flushed. He noted that her hair was in a long pigtail down her back, and he wondered again what it would look like if she freed it.

"Please go," she repeated nervously.

He didn't want to leave. He was genuinely worried about her. "Get a checkup, at least," he said.

"I'll gladly do that, but not tonight. Now, can I please go to bed...?"

He made a rough sound and turned on his heel. "If you don't feel better in the morning, stay home," he said gruffly.

"Don't presume to give me orders," she said calmly. "I'll do what I please."

He glanced over his shoulder at her. She'd blended into the woodwork for most of the time he'd known her. But nothing could disguise the fact that she was a woman, with spirit and independence and intelligence. Isadora had yielded to his will, flattered his

ego, stroked his passions at first until she obsessed
him. But she hadn't been intelligent and she never
fought face-to-face. She was given to pouting and
self-inflicted illnesses to gain sympathy. And she
would never have soiled her hands with a wet kitten…
His own thoughts shocked him. How could he be so
disloyal to the only woman he'd ever loved?

"Good night," he said tersely. He went out the
door and paused just for an instant. "Lock this behind
me."

She glared at his retreating back. She slammed the
door and then locked it. She leaned against the wall,
barely able to get her breath. Her knees were weak.
Why had he come to see her? Was it really a guilty
conscience that had prompted his visit? She couldn't
imagine what would have brought him to her door.
He hated her so much that she'd never expected him
to come to her home. He never had before.

On his way home again, Ramon was wondering
about his motives, too. He kept seeing the spartan
way she lived, the lack of frills, the frugal furnishings.
She was obviously living on her salary, without any
help at all from her aunt and uncle. Was that by
choice, or did they simply ignore her now that Isadora
was gone? He couldn't forget that they'd blamed her
as much as he had for his wife's fatal illness.

He worried the question so much that the next time
he saw the Kensingtons, at a business dinner, he
asked them point-blank about the way Noreen lived.

"She earns a good living," Mary Kensington said
haughtily. "Besides, we don't owe Noreen a thing.
She's responsible for Isadora's death. How can you
care how she lives?"

"She had a stray kitten in the apartment."

Mary waved a hand. "Noreen and those filthy animals! She was forever bringing things home to us. I can't even remember how many trips we made to the local veterinarian."

"She was always too softhearted," Hal Kensington agreed. "She got that from my brother," he reminisced sadly. "He was softhearted, too."

Ramon's dark eyes narrowed. "Then why would such a softhearted woman deliberately leave a sick cousin to die?"

They both looked stunned.

"You hadn't thought about that, had you?" he asked them quietly. "Now ask yourselves one more question. Is Noreen, a qualified nurse, callous enough to let any human being die, much less one she cared about?"

The couple only looked back at him, without speaking. Two years after the fact, they were finally able to think rationally. Perhaps just after Isadora's death, they hadn't really thought at all.

"Have you seen her lately?" he asked them.

"We invited her over for coffee the week before my husband's birthday," Mary admitted. "People were beginning to talk... Why?" she asked abruptly.

"I think she's ill," Ramon said. "Her color is bad, and she seems to become breathless at the least exertion. Do you know if she has a family physician?"

"She hasn't lived at home for a long time," Mary said, "so we don't know much about her private life."

"Has she ever had a complete physical?"

They both looked blank. "Well, she was always so

healthy, there never seemed any need to go to the bother," Mary replied, sounding almost defensive.

He didn't question them further. But he wondered, and that prompted him to go to a friend in the insurance office at the hospital and ask if a complete physical had been required of Noreen when she was accepted by the hospital's nursing department.

"Well, yes, she was supposed to," the officer agreed, "but I don't see it here." He frowned over the computer screen. "Maybe it's somewhere else..."

"Never mind," he said, giving up. "I don't suppose there was anything there."

"If there was, the new laws wouldn't permit us to exclude her on the basis of a preexisting condition" he was reminded.

"Yes, of course."

He thanked the man and left, silently promising himself that he was going to get to the bottom of Noreen's odd behavior and any health secrets she might be harboring.

He couldn't examine her forcibly, but he could observe her. He spent more time at O'Keefe during the next week. He could do it without attracting undue attention because he had several recovering patients there.

He managed to stand close to Noreen while they were going over Mrs. Green's chart. He could hear the breathless sound of her voice, see the flutter of her pulse against the collar of her blouse. Her pallor was evident now, along with the dark circles under her eyes and the weakness that manifested itself in her lack of animation.

But despite his noble motives, it slowly dawned on

him that Noreen was excited by his proximity. He remembered the teasing statement she'd once made about his closeness being the reason for her fast heartbeat. He hadn't taken it seriously. But it seemed to be the truth. She reacted visibly to him, and not only because of whatever illness was beginning to show in her.

It disturbed him because he seemed as vulnerable as she did. He found himself noticing the elegance of her long-fingered hands, the blemishless skin on her oval face, the delicate shape of her mouth. He'd forced himself to never pay attention to her while Isadora was alive, but slowly he began to remember things about Noreen. How she'd blushed when he looked at her, even indifferently. How she avoided him when she was living with Isadora's parents. How she never seemed able to speak to him except on the job. She'd betrayed her feelings for him in a hundred ways over the years, and he'd deliberately avoided noticing.

Until now.

He met her eyes, unblinking, and watched the pupils dilate. She was vulnerable and he wanted to protect her. He hadn't felt that way with Isadora. He'd wanted his wife obsessively, loved her, but she wasn't the woman she'd pretended to be while he was courting her. After they'd married they'd argued incessantly about her need for company, for parties and social gatherings. She'd refused to even discuss Ramon's hunger for a child. Isadora hadn't wanted the responsibility of children. He scowled as he remembered these things.

"You needn't glower at me," Noreen muttered, averting her gaze protectively to the chart she was holding. "I haven't been late on any more medications."

"It wasn't that," he said slowly. His eyes fell to the unsteady rhythm of her jacket, mirroring her heavy heartbeat.

She stepped a little away from him, because the contact with his tall, elegant body disturbed her so. "Were there any other charts you wanted to go over?" she asked unsteadily.

He stuck his hands into the pockets of his lab coat and stared at her without smiling. "I want you to see your family physician and have a complete physical," he said suddenly, bringing her shocked eyes up to meet his. "You're ill and trying to hide it. But it won't work. You can't possibly go on like this."

She was all but speechless as she gaped at him. "I...I've had a checkup," she stammered, floored by his interest in her state of health.

"And...?" he prompted.

"My doctor said that I needed more B-12 in my diet and he gave me a bottle of iron pills," she lied.

He scowled. "That doesn't explain this." He touched her throat lightly, where the pulse jumped erratically.

She jerked back from him, so disturbed by his touch that she flushed red. "Dr. Cortero." She choked out his name. "I'm not obliged to share my physical condition with you. You're not my doctor!"

"No, but I am on staff here," he replied shortly. "I'm ordering you to have another checkup, and I warn you that I'm going to request a copy of the report. You're jeopardizing not only the patients in your care, but your own health by putting this off."

She wished that she had a comeback. He was much

too perceptive. She knew that it wasn't on her account that he was concerned. He didn't want anything to happen to his patients. How amusing, to let herself think for an instant that Dr. Cortero would ever look at her with the tenderness and concern he'd shown to his beloved wife.

She stared down at her white lace-up shoes. "All right," she said wearily, tired of fighting the inevitable. "You win."

"This isn't a contest," he said solemnly.

"Isn't it?" she asked, her tone weary with pain and defeat. "I'll get in touch with my doctor."

"I'm glad you're willing to see reason."

"Don't worry," she said, looking up at him. "I won't deliberately jeopardize your patients."

He scowled. "That isn't why…"

"Please excuse me," she said formally. "I have a lot to do before I can go off duty."

She took the chart and walked to the nurses' station, without looking back.

Ramon watched her go with mixed feelings. He was more confused than he'd ever been before.

Noreen didn't allow herself to watch him leave the ward. She'd spent so many years eating her heart out for him that she took his contempt for her as a matter of course. If he was concerned for her health, it was only because of his patients, and she'd better remember it. She was far too old for pipe dreams.

On the other hand, he was right about her condition. She was only delaying the inevitable. She went home and phoned her surgeon in Macon. She arranged to go into the hospital the following week for the surgery.

Five

Noreen had a cup of black coffee for breakfast. She had to go to work, but she didn't know how she was going to make it through another day. She went to the bathroom mirror and looked at her pale, pinched face. The irregular heartbeat was much worse today. Her breath rattled when she breathed, and it was hard to get a decent breath. It was probably just as well that she'd given in on the subject of the valve replacement. She glanced down at the kitten following her and remembered that she was going to have to find someone to keep him while she was away. That would be her first priority today. She refused to think about her finances for the moment.

She leaned against the sink and lowered her head. It was hard to think straight when she could hear her own heartbeat in her ears, erratic and a little frightening.

Her surgeon had assured her that it was a fairly simple operation these days, that people had it all the time. She was in good health and a fighter, he knew she'd come through it just fine.

Of course she would, she told herself. She certainly would. In the back of her mind, she wished that she could have asked Ramon to do it. He was the very best in his field. But she didn't think he'd consent even if she asked him. He hated her far too much.

She went out the door and everything started going wrong at once. Her car wouldn't start, not for the first time in memory. She heard the sickening sound of the battery going completely dead, and remembered that the mechanic who'd jumped the car to start it just recently had warned her to replace it. She'd been saving up to do that, hoping it would last just a bit longer. She groaned, checking her watch. She'd have to run to catch the bus and she was already late.

She locked the car door and slammed it shut angrily, forgetting in her haste that she'd left the keys in it, and her purse. She stared at her bag through the glass with a sense of despair. Her wallet, her credit cards, her apartment keys, everything she had was in there.

Well, first things first, she decided. This was a good neighborhood and the owners of the apartment house where she lived looked out for her car and the medical student's. She'd worry about her car and purse later.

She had on her raincoat, which contained all the money she would need for bus fare on Marta and snacks at work. She could do without her makeup, or borrow some at the hospital when she needed it. She wouldn't need her keys until she got back home, and anyway, the owner had a passkey and he and his wife lived downstairs.

She trudged out to the street, made it breathlessly to the crowded bus stop on the corner and climbed aboard the bus that would take her right past the hospital where she worked.

It was another cold and rainy morning. With her mind on getting to work on time, she hadn't noticed that the breathlessness, which usually passed, hadn't. She could barely breathe. Her heartbeat felt different. Strange. Frightening.

She saw the people around her as a blur that became brighter and brighter and then, suddenly, vanished.

Ramon was already scrubbed at St. Mary's when they brought the emergency patient into the operating room. A Jane Doe, he thought irritably, on whom he'd have no background information whatsoever. One of his colleagues had already done a catherization. That had indicated a leaky heart valve, which had, over time, deteriorated past saving. He would have to replace it with a prosthetic valve and hope that the unknown woman had no medical conditions that would complicate his surgery. He had no idea of her medications or her state of physical health beyond the heart problems he could see for himself. It was always a risk to operate on a stranger, he thought, but he had no choice.

The oxygen mask was already over her face when his team was assembled and he was ready to begin. Her skin was creamy, very pink and soft, and he regretted the long scar this surgery would leave after he opened and closed the chest cavity.

The surgery took almost four hours. Ramon straightened his back with a grunt at the end of it, satisfied not only with the surgery, but with the closure of the incision he'd made. She'd only have a slight scar. Later, he could recommend a good plastic surgeon, if she could afford it. He knew nothing about her circumstances. She might be a street person, for all he knew. The only part of her he saw was her creamy, soft skin. She had a strong heart and her lungs were in excellent condition, except for a mild bronchitis. She seemed in good health otherwise.

She was taken away to the intensive care unit and he went on to the next case, without giving the identity of his patient another thought for the moment.

Hours later, still in his surgical greens, he went to ICU to have a look at the young woman his skill had saved. She was hooked up to the usual machines and the huge breathing tube of the heart-lung machine was still in her mouth. But when he paused at the side of the bed, his own heart almost stopped. He choked on his own breath. A technician was staring at him with open curiosity. He knew the blood had drained out of his face. That was Noreen. And she'd collapsed with a damaged heart valve. She had a bad heart, and he hadn't known. Nobody had known!

Shaken out of his normal calm, he motioned for the floor nurse to join him. "I was told that this woman's identity was unknown!" he said harshly.

"She had no identification on her at all," the nurse began.

"She's my late wife's cousin!" he raged, his fist clenched at his side. "I would never have performed surgery on her if I'd had any idea in the world who she was!"

She felt the whip of his anger and winced. "I'm sure if anyone had known... We thought she was an indigent—"

"She's a nurse." He interrupted irritably. "She works at O'Keefe's in the cardiac care unit." Even while he spoke the words, he was remembering his own unjust treatment of her when she'd been desperately ill and hiding it. He hated remembering how unfair he'd been to her. She might have died...

"But how did she get here?" the nurse was asking. "And without any identification on her? Surely she had a wallet?"

"I don't know." He stared down at her white, drawn face, expressionless from the anesthesia. He glanced at her small hand, from which tubes rose above the shunts. The nails were short, rounded, unvarnished. She had elegant, but capable hands. She had a bad heart, a damaged valve. She hadn't told him. Why? Had she truly been afraid to let him operate on her, afraid that in his contempt and dislike, he might fail her? It was sheer torture to think about it!

"I'll see if I can find out how she came to be here," the nurse assured him.

"Never mind," he said shortly, turning on his heel impatiently. "I'll find out myself. Let me know if there's any change, any change at all."

"Yes, sir."

He paused to check another of his surgical patients and then, with a last worried glance toward Noreen, went down to the emergency room.

It took several minutes to discover that Noreen had collapsed on a Marta bus and had been brought to the emergency room by ambulance without a scrap of identification on her. Possibly when she'd passed out, someone had taken her purse, he surmised.

The clothes she'd been wearing were in a plastic bag. He took them out to his car when he went, with plans to return them to her apartment. He didn't have a key, so he found the owner of the apartment house instead.

"Locked her keys in her car this morning, I noticed," the man said dryly. "Purse and all. I saw her take off after that Marta bus. She had to run to catch up with it. I expect she's upset."

"She had a close call," Ramon said curtly. "She had heart surgery this morning. She won't be home for several days."

The owner was shocked. "Such a quiet, nice young woman," he remarked. "Always had a kind word for everyone, and a smile. She'll be missed. Please tell her that my wife and I wish her the best, and we'll look after the apartment until she gets back. Anything you want from her apartment?"

"Later, perhaps. I'll be back to get anything she needs after I've spoken to her." He'd not only have to do that, but he'd have to do something about that kitten, too. It would die if he left it. Besides, she hadn't wanted the apartment owner to know she had it. Pets were against the rules.

"I'll be around, if I'm needed. You a relative?" he asked.

"Yes," Ramon said without explanation.

He left, with the intention of driving himself home for dinner. But he couldn't. Involuntarily he turned back in the direction of the hospital.

She hadn't regained consciousness. It wasn't unusual, but it worried Ramon. He checked her carefully with the stethoscope, noting the steady rhythm of her brand-new metal valve, which made a soft *chink-chink* sound as it opened and closed. The valve would last for many years, and her quality of life would be enhanced by it. No more breathlessness at the slightest exertion, no more erratic heart rhythms, no more fatigue.

He frowned, wondering when she'd first known about it. Surely she'd had some sort of warning and had seen a doctor when she started having trouble. Judging from the condition the valve was in, she had to have noticed that something was wrong. Her bad color alone had alerted him to a physical problem.

That line of curiosity led him further along. He sat in the cafeteria, eating without tasting his food, and his mind continued its meandering. Why had she never told anyone of her condition? Had she had some violent episode with it? Did her aunt and uncle know anything was wrong? Did they care?

He couldn't help noticing the difference in the way the Kensingtons had treated Noreen since Isadora's death. Like himself, they'd blamed her for that. None of them had ever considered anything save neglect as the cause of Isadora's untimely passing. But Noreen's present condition opened the whole subject up again.

He finished his meal and got up to take his tray to the moving belt assembly in the canteen, frowning thoughtfully. He put it down and then checked his watch. It was going on eight hours since he'd operated on Noreen.

He went back up on the staff elevator to the ICU, and moved right along past the automatic door to the cubicle where Noreen was settled.

With a rough sigh, he went into her small cubicle and checked the many monitors to which she was connected. She seemed to be in acceptable ranges on all of them. But why hadn't she regained consciousness?

He leaned over her. "Noreen," he called abruptly.

And all at once, her eyes flew open.

His heart jumped at the unexpected but welcome response. Her eyes followed his dark face curiously, as if she wasn't quite conscious even now. Probably she wasn't. The effects of anesthesia lingered.

He checked her pupils, borrowed a stethoscope from one of the nurses and listened, nodding, to the steady rhythm of her heart. Her lungs sounded clearer.

He lifted his head and searched her eyes, noting that they'd removed the breathing tube from her mouth.

She tried to swallow. "So...dry." Her voice sounded weak and shaky.

He found one of the swabs kept for moistening the lips, drew it out of a sterile package and applied it to the inside of her mouth.

"It's the anesthetic we use," he explained. "It leaves a bad taste in the mouth and some dryness. It will pass."

She seemed to relax. "What are...you doing here?" she managed drowsily.

"No one knew who you were when you were brought into surgery," he explained. "I operated."

She frowned. "Unethical," she whispered.

He shrugged. "Yes. But I didn't see your face. I had no idea it was you."

She was having a hard time keeping her eyes open. "Dr. Myers will...be...upset."

"Myers?" he asked.

"In...Macon. County General. He was...supposed to operate...next week."

She lapsed into sleep again, weary from the surgery and the exertion of talking. She was in pain, too, from the surgery. The nurses had given her the painkiller he'd already ordered.

He moved away from the bed with a quiet sigh, pausing since he was in the unit to check on his other patient.

She'd sleep the rest of the night; he was fairly sure of that. He went home and, on an impulse, sought a telephone number for a cardiac surgeon in Macon named Myers.

He found the man without too much difficulty. When Dr. Myers knew to whom he was speaking, he was stunned.

"I've heard of you," he told Ramon on the telephone. "You're quite well-known." He paused. "Is this about a patient of mine?"

"My late wife's cousin, Noreen Kensington," Ramon began.

"Ah, Norie," he replied, a smile in his voice. "Hard girl to get on the table, if you know what I mean. I happened to be visiting an old friend in an exclusive Atlanta apartment house two years ago when the superintendent found a young woman collapsed on the staircase and asked for my help after he'd phoned for an ambulance. I checked her over and went with her to a local hospital and conferred with the emergency room doctor about her. He ordered X-rays and we saw immediately that something was wrong. He admitted her, barely conscious and confused, and we did an echocardiogram.'' He sighed. ''The valve was leaking a little, and I recommended surgery, but she was lucid enough to refuse. She kept mumbling something about her cousin, who was apparently under the weather, and how she needed to get back there. I thought her own condition merited more concern, so I had her sedated and kept her overnight, until she was stabilized.''

While Isadora died. Ramon's eyes closed. So it hadn't been negligence at all. Noreen had collapsed.

''Was it a heart attack?'' he asked.

''I think it might have been a very mild one, although nothing showed up on the EKG or the echocardiogram. She recovered and refused surgery, but I insisted on keeping a watchful eye on her. I had her come to see me every three months. About a month ago, the leaking began to increase and I insisted that she arrange to have surgery before the situation became critical. She was already showing symptoms...'' There was a pause, as if Ramon's very silence communicated something to him. ''How is she?''

''She collapsed on a Marta bus this morning. She'd locked her purse in her car and ran to catch the bus to work, but she never got there. They brought her to my hospital as a Jane Doe and I performed emergency surgery on her, without realizing her identity until the procedure was complete.''

''Well, she had the best care, whatever the circumstances. It's a relief to me to know that she's in such good hands. She's going to be all right?''

''Her vitals are within acceptable ranges,'' Ramon said, ''and she's conscious. We'll have to wait and see how she does. I expect a complete recovery.'' He took a slow breath. "I never knew she had a heart condition. I wasn't told."

"Don't feel bad. She never told anyone," he replied. "I gather that she's an independent young woman with no close family."

"She has an aunt and uncle who took her in when her parents died…"

"Of course, but you know how it is when some relatives wind up with unexpected kids. They never quite consider them their own."

Ramon was still trying to get over the shock. "She told you that she was living with her cousin's parents?"

"Yes. She'd applied for a passport and had her birth certificate with her when she came to my office the last time. She was thinking of taking a job overseas, in some third-world country, she said. Thank God this happened before she left the States."

Ramon sat down. "Yes."

"Well, I'm happy to hear that my patient is going to survive. Please tell her that I'd like to see her when she's back on her feet again."

"I'll do that. Thank you for what you've done for her."

"I did nothing except make her come for checkups."

"You kept her alive. Come and see me when you're in Atlanta next time. I'm at St. Mary's."

"I'll do that. You might, uh, return the favor if you're ever in Macon."

Ramon chuckled. "I'll make a point of it. Good evening."

He hung up and the smile faded. What a lot he

didn't know about Noreen. He wondered if the Kensingtons knew about her heart.

He had to find out. He phoned their number, only
to get an answering machine message that they were
out of town and wouldn't be back until the following
week.

He borrowed the passkey from the owner after he
had a locksmith get Norie's car unlocked for him. He
paid the locksmith and sent him on his way. Then,
with a wave to the owner of the apartment house, he
took her purse inside and unlocked the door of her
apartment on the second floor. The kitten came running to meet him, probably half-starved, he thought
as he picked it up and tucked it under his jacket, so
that no one would see him take it with him as he
locked the apartment up again and left.

He had to stop by the store on the way home to
buy a few necessary items for the kitten. It was a
well-mannered little thing, he thought. It laid down
beside him on the front seat and just stayed there,
purring happily, not bothering anything.

When he got home again, it was company for him.
He hadn't realized how lonely his apartment was. He
made himself a pot of coffee, settled into an easy
chair with a steaming cup beside him on the table and
opened the medical journal that he'd received that
day. The kitten climbed up into his lap, curled itself
comfortably and went to sleep purring.

Before he went to bed, he telephoned ICU to check
on Noreen, and found that she was continuing to
make progress. When he went to bed, the kitten
tagged right along. He felt it beside his head on the
pillow as he drifted off to sleep.

* * *

It was late the next day before he was able to get back into ICU to check on Noreen. His schedule had been hectic all day, and he was between surgeries when he paused by her bed, still in his surgical greens.

Without a word, he checked her over, studied the monitors and listened to her chest.

"I'm...all right. When can I go home?" she asked.

He cocked an eyebrow. "Funny girl."

"They won't give me anything to drink," she accused. "And that short blond nurse ignores every question I ask her."

"I'll have her shot," he promised agreeably. "You're being moved out of here in the morning to a private room. I'll engage a nurse to sit with you."

"I don't need—" she winced and paused to breath, "—help from...you!"

"Thank you. I like you, too." He searched the angry pale eyes and smiled reluctantly. "Yes, you're definitely better. I'll be back to check on you later."

She blinked, still a little hungover from the anesthesia.

"Go to sleep," he said gently.

She closed her eyes obediently.

He turned to the small blond nurse and motioned her to join him by the door.

"I know," she said, holding up a hand, "I'm the wicked witch of ICU and I've been torturing her." She smiled apologetically. "She wants cracked ice every five minutes. I have two patients who aren't doing half as well as she is, and medications to take around, we're shorthanded by one nurse..."

He patted her on the shoulder. "Take two aspirins

and call me in the morning," he told her. "You'll be fine."

He left before she could get her mouth closed.

The last surgery went poorly. The patient was so far gone that all Ramon's skill wasn't enough to save him. He went out to tell the family, empty inside as he saw their grief and was helpless to do anything about it. One of the female chaplains appeared out of nowhere and took charge of the devastated family. Thank God for the chaplains, he thought as he went to change clothes. They were worth their weight in diamonds.

He made one more trip to ICU that night. The shifts had changed and a bright and cheerful young African-American nurse was in charge. She gave him a big grin.

"Your patients are going out on the floor tomorrow, aren't they?" she asked.

"You tell me," he replied. "Think they'll do?"

She nodded. "They're improving by leaps and bounds. We fed Miss Kensington her supper tonight and she ate all of it. Great appetite."

He smiled. "Good for her. No deterioration?"

She shook her head. "Her vitals are good and getting better by the minute."

"Thanks." He went to stand by Noreen's bed. She was awake fully now, and aware of her surroundings.

"You operated on me," she accused.

"I told you before, I didn't know who you were. You had no identification on you."

"I locked my purse in the car and had to run to catch the bus." She drew in a labored breath and touched her chest through the hospital gown. "Hurts."

"They'll give you something for that," he said. "Running for the bus probably precipitated this. Do you remember how you felt when you collapsed?"

"I didn't feel anything," she recalled. "I saw the floor coming up toward me and I thought, I'll break my nose. Then everything went white."

"No pain?"

"Not that I remember." She searched his drawn face. "You look so tired," she said involuntarily.

It surprised him that his heart jumped at her gentle concern. "Long day," he said tersely. "And I lost a patient."

"I'm sorry."

Not one expression escaped his control. "It goes with the job. But it always hurts." He searched her face. "Your color's much better."

"When can I go back to work?"

"When you're well."

She glowered at him. "I'll starve if I don't work."

"No, you won't. Your hospital insurance is the best in town, and it has a disability clause."

"How did you know?"

"I checked. You're already on the computer. I signed you in. By the way, I tried to call your aunt and uncle, but they're out of town."

Her eyes shifted to the curtain. "There's no need to bother them. They don't like hospitals."

"You're their niece," he said. "They care about you."

She didn't answer. She knew better, but she wasn't going to discuss it with him. He should have expected it.

"You're going out to 3 East tomorrow," he said.

"The cardiac ward. All private rooms. There's a nursing shortage. I'll lie there and die and nobody will notice."

"Not there, you won't. You'll be hooked to the monitor at the desk. Someone watches constantly. And the technicians are all over the ward. You'll be fine. All the same, I'm having a nurse special you."

She glared at him. "I can't afford…!"

"Calm down. Don't put any stress on that new valve," he cautioned. "And I can afford it. You're family."

"No, I'm not." She ground out the words. "No relation. None."

He saw the resentment and hostility in her eyes, and knew that she had every right to feel it. For two years he'd blamed her for something she hadn't done. She'd tried to explain at first and he'd refused to listen. Probably he deserved her contempt.

He stuck his hands into his pockets. "Have it your way. But you'll get the private nurse, all the same. I'll check on you in the morning."

She was full of things to tell him, but he didn't stay to listen. She watched his broad back disappear out the door and her fist hit the bed furiously. The action hurt her chest and she groaned.

"Need something for pain?"

"Yes, please," she answered the pretty nurse. She almost asked if they had anything for a dark-eyed pain in the neck, but considering how the staff adored Ramon here, she felt it was more diplomatic to keep her mouth shut.

He hadn't been joking about the nurse, she discovered the next day. Just after supper, a plump little tornado came in and sat down with a bag of knitting. She introduced herself as Miss Polly Plimm. She was a nurse who'd worked on special cases for Ramon before. This young woman would need some assistance for a day or two, she noted, and she was more than happy to have the work. Having retired the year before, her lack of industry was beginning to atrophy her bones. She fetched cracked ice for Noreen and checked her vital signs and the catheter bag periodically, and encouraged her young charge at every turn.

Brad stopped by to check on his friend and was delighted to find her in such good hands. He was on day shift now and came to visit with her each evening for a few minutes before he went off duty. He noted her progress and applauded it, but he worried about what was going to happen when she had to go home. She was already talking about going back to her apartment. He hoped the surgeon wasn't going to allow that. She really couldn't stay by herself.

Six

Noreen was more aware of her surroundings after her second day on the cardiac ward, and her first totally logical thought was of the poor kitten, alone in her apartment. She and nurse Plimm walked around the unit two times, while she brooded about the poor kitten that she'd forgotten under the effect of the surgery and the anesthetic.

Brad came by to see her and waited while she was settled and hooked up again to the oxygen and IV and cardiac monitor.

"My kitten," she said plaintively. "She's alone in my apartment. She's been there for days with no food and no water. She'll be dead!"

"Ah, the kitten," Brad mused. "Well, she's something of a legend already, from what I hear. She's rooming with Dr. Cortero."

Her heart skipped beats. She gaped at him. "With Ramon?"

"The very same. Imagine that. I thought he hated animals."

"So did I."

"You'd never believe it, to hear him talk about that cat. He's bought it a collar and all sorts of toys and it sleeps with him."

"You're right. I don't believe it. You're pulling my leg."

"Ask him when he does rounds," he returned wryly. "I dare you."

Noreen took the information with a large grain of salt. Isadora had once told her that Ramon hated domestic animals and wouldn't want anything with fur and claws around him. She'd also said that Ramon didn't like children and had no intention of siring any. He liked parties and social gatherings and he was a neatness freak at home, Isadora had added carelessly.

He hadn't seemed that way to Noreen, but she didn't really know him. He'd made sure of that. The only person who ever managed to get close to him was Isadora. Since her death, he was completely alone. He didn't even date.

That didn't surprise Noreen, because she was well aware of his obsession for Isadora. All her life, the older girl had been the apple of everyone's eye. There was no love left over for Noreen at the Kensington home, because it all went to Isadora. That was still true, even though Isadora was long dead.

Miss Plimm had gone down to the cafeteria to get her supper. Noreen, momentarily alone, was so lost in her own thoughts that she didn't hear Ramon come in. He was bending over her with a stethoscope when she noticed him, and she jumped, startled.

"Don't do that," he muttered impatiently, sliding the cold metal against her chest under the loose hospital gown. "Breathe normally."

That was difficult, with his face so close. She kept her eyes shut, so that she wouldn't have to see that dark complexion, the thickness of his straight black hair, the liquid black of his eyes. She couldn't bear to look at him. It hurt too much.

He drew away, watching her eyes open. They didn't quite meet his.

"I'm doing fine," she informed him.

"Yes, I know." He shoved his hands into his pockets. "How's your appetite?"

"I eat everything that's put before me."

"No, you don't," he replied. "You eat the Jell-O and soup and leave everything else. That can't continue. You have to have protein."

"I have gas," she replied with mild belligerence. "There's no room inside for food."

"I'll write up something to take care of that." He made a notation on the chart. "Eat, or I'll have to keep you on intravenous fluids."

"All right," she said heavily. She glanced up and away again. "How's my kitten?" she asked.

He smiled, his dark eyes twinkling. "She eats like two cats."

She stared at his jacket. "Thank you for looking after her."

"She's no trouble."

"I can't believe that. I know you don't like animals." Or me, she added silently.

He scowled. Perhaps she wasn't quite recovered

from the confusion brought on by the anesthesia. He
liked animals. He lived alone because he hadn't had
enough time to devote to one, and an apartment was
hardly suited to dogs and cats.

"How's the pain?" he asked.

"I'm doing fine," she repeated.

He hesitated. She wouldn't look at him and she
didn't seem inclined to talk. He picked up her hand
to examine the shunts they'd inserted in her veins to
connect to the fluids she was being given. He
scowled.

"When were these shunts flushed last? Meredith
always dates them so they don't remain in place
longer than three days."

"Meredith didn't do these," she replied. "I think
Annie did. I know they haven't been in longer than
a day."

He made a note on the chart to have them flushed.
One seemed to be clogged. The shunts were im-
planted so that if there was an emergency, a nurse
wouldn't have to scramble to find a vein for the nee-
dle. Keeping them free of clogs was essential to post-
surgical heart patients. He picked up her other hand,
noting the softness of it, the short, clean nails, the
silky skin behind her knuckles.

"You must use hand cream constantly," he remarked as his thumb smoothed over the back of her
hand. "Your skin is incredibly soft."

She pulled her hand back from his. She still
wouldn't look at him. "They're working hands," she
replied, "not model's hands."

"I know that, Noreen."

He hardly ever called her by name if he could avoid
it. Didn't he know that he was torturing her? She

closed her eyes, praying that he'd go away and leave her alone.

It was all too apparent that she was going to shut him out. She'd been hurt too much over the years to warm to him now. He scowled, because it bothered him that Noreen hated his touch. He remembered her at his first anniversary party, backing away from him in the kitchen. It had bothered him even then, even when he was married.

"I'll check on you later."

"Thanks, but there's no need. Miss Plimm is very efficient."

Her remoteness irritated him. "Would you rather I sent John on rounds?" he asked curtly, naming an associate in his surgical group.

"That…might be better, if you don't mind," she said in a subdued tone.

His temper flared, hot and unreasonable. Without another word, he carried her chart back to its tray, slipped it in and left the ward.

Noreen sighed her relief. Just a few more days, she told herself, and she could get out of here. When she was recovered, she'd look for a job at a hospital in the suburbs, one where Ramon wasn't on staff. She owed him her life, but not her soul. She wasn't going to put herself through any more torment on his behalf. She recalled applying for a passport some months earlier, with some half-formed notion of sacrificing her nursing talent in some third-world nation to escape thoughts of Ramon. It seemed ridiculous in light of what had happened to her. At the time, it had seemed very rational.

She stared blankly out the window, wondering if her aunt and uncle were really out of town. Ramon had probably been softening the blow. They'd never wanted Noreen in the first place. They'd only taken her in from a sense of responsibility, not out of love. She'd been an extra person in their lives, always on the outside of the family circle, always the fifth wheel. It had hurt when she was a little girl, but she'd grown accustomed to being excluded from family pastimes and assigned to endless domestic tasks. Since Isadora's death, they'd only invited her to the house once, and it had been far too uncomfortable for all of them to repeat. She didn't need to be told that they'd only invited her out of a sense of duty, to keep people who knew them from gossiping.

She sighed and closed her eyes. She was going to start her life over, she decided. She was going to stop pining for Ramon and regretting the indifference of her aunt and uncle and everyone blaming her for Isadora's death. She was going to get a new job, a new wardrobe, a new apartment and a new life. Now that she'd be healthy and whole again, she could plan on a future. She was going to live it to the fullest.

Ramon, unaware of her plotting, stormed into his apartment after work with a face like a thundercloud. He was furious that Noreen didn't want him to visit her, to oversee her care. He'd saved her life—didn't that matter to her?

He poured himself a drink and sat down heavily in his armchair, instantly joined by the kitten. It curled up against him and purred.

"At least you're glad to see me," he murmured, stroking it absently.

He'd enjoyed the kitten's company. It made him think of all he'd missed in his life. He came home to an empty apartment, to loneliness and grief and isolation. When Isadora had been alive, he came home to noise and laughter and a roomful of people, because she liked parties and gave them frequently. He never had peace or the luxury of silence in which to read the medical journals that Isadora despised.

He wondered now if she'd needed the companionship of other people to make up for the emptiness in her life with Ramon. Isadora hadn't liked animals and children. He could still hear her laughter when he'd suggested starting a family. Ruin her figure and be a slave to an infant, she'd exclaimed, what sane woman would give up her independence to be a little homemaker? As for animals, she wouldn't have cat hair on her elegant furniture, and dogs were just too much trouble. Like children.

He'd loved Isadora, so he'd given up his dreams of domesticity after that one conversation. But he saw his colleagues with their wives and children, heard them plan vacations at resorts that catered to families. He'd been envious, because he and Isadora had parties instead of a family. They grew apart after the first few months of their marriage and went their separate ways. And in the last few months before her death, Isadora had been drinking far too much. She cheated on him, made threats, impossible demands, accusations. She hadn't been happy. She'd promised to do herself in if he went off to France without her, depriving her of seeing her lover who was also going to be there.

He'd refused because of her health, not out of jealousy. But his reason hadn't mattered to Isadora. She'd raged at him that he was only a dog in the manger. It was Noreen he lusted after, she'd accused wildly, and not for the first time. Well, Noreen would never want him, because she was afraid of men and especially him, she'd raged. She'd never explained, and he hadn't wondered about the statement. Until now.

He sipped his drink, recalling other incidents, other arguments, that belied the perfect marriage he and Isadora had shown to the world. She hated his work, his commitment to his patients, his absences in emergencies. Once, she'd hung up on a patient's hysterical wife, refusing to call Ramon to the telephone. The man had been in cardiac arrest, and fortunately, another doctor had come to his aid. That had happened a week before Ramon left for France. And Isadora had gone walking in the cold rain without a coat, with bronchitis.

He'd gone to France after having asked Noreen to stay with Isadora and look after her. Noreen had agreed gladly, giving up her free days to take care of her cousin.

Everyone had thought that Noreen let Isadora die. Now, Ramon felt he knew and could accept the truth. It had been a tragic round of circumstances, ending with Noreen's mild heart attack. And he and the Kensingtons hadn't even allowed her to defend herself. They'd blamed her, isolated her, punished her for something that wasn't her fault, for two long years. No wonder she withdrew from Ramon's touch, from his offers of help.

He groaned aloud. How could he have been so arrogantly judgmental? How could he have overlooked Noreen's compassion, branded her as a merciless killer? He was as guilty as she was. He was more guilty. He'd left Isadora behind out of necessity, because she couldn't safely fly in that condition. But only now did he admit that he hadn't wanted to take her with him.

His fairy-tale marriage had been going steadily downhill. He and Isadora had fought constantly at the last, especially on the day he'd left, and his conscience had beaten him over it, again and again. He'd wanted some time to himself. It was his absence as much as Noreen's that had led to Isadora's death, but he hadn't been able to admit his guilt or have anyone know that his blissful marriage was a sort of hell. And now it was too late to make any difference. Noreen wanted no part of him. She never had. She'd backed away from him constantly over the past six years, especially after his marriage to Isadora. How could he blame her?

If only there was still time to make it up to her, he thought sadly. He couldn't take back the past two years, but he could make her life a little easier. He had to talk to the Kensingtons. They had to be made to understand, too. Noreen had been done a great wrong. Now it was up to him to make it right. He hoped he could.

Noreen was able to walk around the unit three times the next day, with Brad lending her his support. She laughed at her own light-headedness, but she kept on, grinning at the nurses as she trundled along. Several of the patients were up walking today. All of them were steadily improving and looking healthier. The stimulation of walking kept the new valve working and helped clear her lungs and build her strength back up. She never doubted that she was going to be able to walk out of here within days. Her pleasure showed in her face.

At least, it did until Ramon came onto the ward and she saw him in her path. Her brilliant smile faded. Her eyes went lackluster and her gaze dropped abruptly to the floor. Her hand clung tight to Brad's long arm.

"Good," Ramon said, ignoring her lack of animation. "Walking is just what you need to do, as often as you can manage. It will make your recovery easier."

"This is our third time around," Brad told him. "She's making progress."

"Yes, so I see."

"We need to move on," she told Brad. "I get wobbly when I stand still."

"Brad, you're needed in 310," one of the nurses called. "Mr. Sharp says his medicine's running out on the breathing machine."

Brad hated to desert her, and his expression reflected it.

"I'll take her the rest of the way around," Ramon said, moving to take Brad's place. "See to your patient."

"Yes, sir," Brad said, casting an apologetic glance at Noreen, who looked as if she'd just been turned over to the headsman.

"It won't kill you to touch me," Ramon said tersely, guiding her hand to his forearm. "Come on. Walk."

She did, hating him, hating the curious glances of the other workers—it was unusual for a surgeon to take time to loiter with a patient while he was doing rounds.

"How's the pain?" he asked as they rounded the nurses' station.

"Better," she said through her teeth.

He only nodded, drawing her along beside him slowly until they were back at her room. He helped her into bed, took off her slippers, unhooked her breathing tube from the oxygen cylinder and refitting it to the wall unit before the technician appeared to do it.

He took his stethoscope and listened to her chest while she struggled with weakness and breathlessness and her own helpless reaction to his proximity.

His black eyes met her light ones at point-blank range. He didn't move at all.

"My chest hurts," she said uneasily.

"I'll have them bring you something for it." He pulled the sheet up to her waist. "Are you warm enough?"

"Yes. Of course." She lowered her eyes to his tie.

She heard his slow, deep intake of breath. "You haven't asked about your kitten."

She was trying desperately to control her breathing. "Is she all right?"

"She's fine. You'll be glad to have her back when you go home."

"Yes."

He smiled faintly. "I've gotten used to her."

"There are plenty of homeless kittens in the world," she said noncommittally.

"I was hoping I might be allowed visitation rights," he replied.

She looked up, then, her eyes devoid of all feeling. "I don't think so," she replied tautly.

His eyelids jerked, ever so slightly. He searched her eyes. "Is this how it's going to be from now on?" he asked quietly.

"I don't know what you mean."

"You know," he replied. "Good God, it must have occurred to you that I'd find out what happened eventually. I was shattered to know you'd had a heart attack and that was why you'd left Isadora alone."

"It did occur to me," she told him. "But perhaps it hasn't occurred to you that I tried to tell you and you wouldn't listen. None of you would let me tell you what happened." Her face closed up completely. "I've been treated like a murderess for two years. Do you think I can just forget all that?"

He stood up straight. "No," he replied. "And I should have realized it." He searched her eyes. "I would apologize," he added quietly. "But too much has happened for a simple apology to wipe out the past two years. I am truly sorry, if it helps."

She lowered her eyelids. She was tired, worn-out. "You didn't know," she said dully. "They didn't know, either. Oh, what difference does it make now?" she added miserably, biting hard on her lower lip. "She's dead! And it was my fault! I should have tried harder to make the doctor understand why I had to go home!"

He felt the words as if they were the twist of a knife in his stomach. "Noreen!" he exclaimed softly.

The door opened and Brad came in, his gaze accusing on Ramon's swarthy face. He moved to her side and glared at the older man. "Can't you stop hurting her?" he asked quietly. "Good God, man, she's been through enough!"

"Yes, she has," Ramon said in a subdued tone, watching the tears roll down Noreen's pale cheeks with pain in his eyes. "And I haven't helped matters." He turned and went to the open doorway. "I'll have them bring her something for the pain. Try to get her to eat.''

Brad didn't answer him. He pulled a tissue from the box at the side table and handed it to Noreen to absorb the tears running down her cheeks. He'd never seen her look so totally defeated.

Ramon went down the hall in a fog. Tears on Noreen's face. He'd seen them before and turned a cold heart to them. Now, it hurt him to have made her cry.

He'd expected to wave his hand and undo years of indifference and hostility. For the first time, he saw what a long road it was going to be, to win back Noreen's trust. It left him numb.

Miss Plimm, the private duty nurse, stayed with Noreen at night for three days, but the following morning Noreen quietly and appreciatively sent her on her way. She wasn't going to be obliged to Ramon for any more expenses, if she could help it.

Feeling that way, it was a good thing she couldn't see ahead to the following Monday, when she was released from the hospital. She'd taken the obligatory nutrition class—the only surgical heart patient who attended it alone—and the nurses had filled out the necessary forms and given her prescriptions and appointment cards for follow-up visits to Ramon's surgical group and the cardiologist.

She waited for the porter to bring a wheelchair and the nurse to get a taxi for her. She hadn't counted on any complications. Well, possibly the kitten, but perhaps the owner of her apartment house would bend the rules for her. He and his wife were compassionate people and they liked her.

It was a shock to find the Kensingtons at the door of the ward when the porter came for her.

She gave them a wary glance, her face stone-cold, without welcome.

"Ramon said that you'd be leaving today," her uncle Hal began.

"Yes, I'm going back to my apartment," she replied. She didn't smile. "Why are you here?"

He looked surprised. "You had major surgery," he said.

"We were on vacation," her aunt added. "We only got back today. If we'd known, certainly we'd have been here…"

"Why bother pretending?" she asked them wearily. "You've made the obligatory visit. No one will gossip about you. Now, if you don't mind, I'm not feeling well. I'd just like to go home."

"You can have your old room," Aunt Mary said hesitantly. "We'll have a nurse stay with you…"

"I'm going to my apartment, Aunt Mary," she replied, averting her eyes.

"But you live alone." Her uncle interrupted. "You can't stay by yourself."

"I've been by myself for years," she said with indifference in her voice, in her eyes, noting their confused expressions. "I prefer it." She nodded to the porter, who began pushing her toward the hall. "Thank you for stopping by," she said, without looking at them as the porter guided her toward the elevator.

The Kensingtons stood side by side, perplexed and disturbed. They'd expected their concern to be welcomed, but this Noreen wasn't the quiet, undemanding, shy little girl they'd taken into their home so many years before.

"Ramon said that she wasn't the same," Mary Kensington told her husband. "I guess we should have allowed for the pain and the distrust. We've treated her very badly."

"All three of us," her husband agreed quietly. "If only we'd listened when she tried to explain. I feel terrible. She had this condition that could have killed her, and we didn't even know."

"We'll bring her around," she said.

He laughed without humor. "Do you think so?" He stuck his hands deep into his pockets. "Let's get something to eat."

She took his arm and they walked to the elevator. The doors were just closing on Noreen when they saw Ramon coming from the staff elevator bank, dressed in an expensive suit.

"Where is she?" he asked when he spotted the Kensingtons.

"Gone downstairs to get a cab," Mr. Kensington said heavily. "She wouldn't even talk to us."

"A cab?" He didn't stay to discuss anything. He sprinted into an elevator going down and made it just before the doors closed.

Down in the lobby, the porter had left Noreen sitting near the desk while he went outside to hail a cab.

Ramon got behind the chair and began to push it toward the entrance, where his car was temporarily parked.

"Wh…what?" Noreen gasped when she realized what he was doing.

"Jack, open this door for me," he called to the porter. "Never mind the cab, I'm taking her home."

"Yes, sir." The young man helped him get a fuming, protesting Noreen into the passenger seat. Ramon took her single suitcase and slid it into the trunk.

"I want to take a cab," she protested when he got in beside her and started the car.

"You'll go where you're told," he said, his faint Spanish accent suddenly noticeable as he pulled the vehicle out of the hospital entrance and onto the small service road that led to the highway.

"Not with you!" she said angrily.

"Calmate," he said softly. "Be quiet. You won't do yourself any good by losing your temper."

She did feel rough. She sat back against the seat with her eyes closed, fighting down nausea and pain. It had been a turbulent morning.

"Did you send them here?" she asked when they were on the expressway.

"The Kensingtons?" he asked. "No. I knew they'd be back today, so I called to ask if they knew you'd had surgery. They were pretty shocked."

"Why?"

He glanced at her. "You appeared to be healthy when you lived at home."

"It was never home," she replied, staring out the window.

He was silent, his brooding gaze on traffic as he drove. "You always seemed to blend in with the woodwork."

"Of course I did," she sighed. "I was a stick of furniture. I've lived in the shadows for most of my adult life. That's going to change. When I'm back on my feet, I may go abroad to work. I'm going to leave everything behind and start over."

His heart jumped. He hadn't thought she might

leave town. He realized with a start that he didn't want her to go. It was a surprising sensation, like stepping out into space. He glanced at her with quizzical dark eyes.

"You won't do anything for three months," he said flatly. "I've put a lot of work into getting you on your feet. I won't let you undo it."

"For three months, I'll do what I'm told," she agreed. "After that, I'm going to do what I please."

"You'll need to have regular checkups," he said pointedly. "You'll have to take blood thinners and a cardiac regulator. The medicine will have to be monitored closely."

"I'll make sure I have a good doctor."

He lapsed into silence. Minutes later, he pulled up at the entrance to his apartment building and signaled the doorman to get the suitcase out of the open trunk. He picked up Noreen, purse and papers and all, and strode into the building.

"What...are you...doing?" she exclaimed, struggling.

"Be still."

He kept walking, aware of the doorman following with the suitcase.

"My cousin is just out of the hospital with open-heart surgery," Ramon told the doorman. "I'm keeping her with me until she's able to stay alone."

"A wise move, sir," the younger man said, smiling as he pushed the button for Ramon's floor. The elevator arrived and the three of them got on.

Noreen was near tears, all over again. She lay helpless in Ramon's strong arms, inhaling the spicy scent of his expensive cologne, her arm stiff across his broad shoulders, as rigid as a board trying not to show how her body reacted to his touch.

It was impersonal, she told herself firmly as he shifted her closer to reinforce his grip. He was doing it because she was some sort of relation, even if distant, and he couldn't afford to have people gossip about her being left alone in her condition. That was why the Kensingtons had come to the hospital. Everybody was so afraid of what people would say.

She wasn't aware that she was crying until she felt Ramon's dark eyes cut down to her face and heard his soft intake of breath.

When the elevator stopped, he strode to his door, letting her down briefly to search for the key and unlock the door. He handed the car keys to the doorman, so that he could park the car.

"Leave them at the desk for me, if you would," he told the man, and taking Noreen's bag from him and putting it in the foyer. "I'll be down shortly."

"Of course, sir. Hope you do well, ma'am." He smiled and nodded to Noreen as Ramon picked her up again, but she was beyond answering.

Ramon carried her into the guest bedroom and placed her gently on the bed. "Stay put." He reached behind her and moved pillows into place to prop her up against.

He went into the next room. Minutes later, he fetched a pitcher of fruit juice, a glass, her medicines and, lastly, the kitten. It sat in her lap and purred loudly.

"Sweet girl," she said through her tears, stroking the cat and smiling wearily.

"She'll keep you company until I get home. I have rounds to make, and patients to see. I'll get back as soon as I can. Meanwhile, the phone is here. If you need anything, call downstairs. I'll arrange to get Miss Plimm back,'' he added, reminding her that she'd dismissed the poor woman without his approval.

"I can't stay here," she began.

"You can't stay alone," he returned. "I'd counted on you going home with the Kensingtons."

"And I wouldn't, so now you're stuck with me, and you don't want to be." The tears fell more hotly than ever. She closed her eyes on a harsh sob. "God in heaven, why couldn't you just...let me go...home?"

Rounds, patients, work, all of it was dismissed in the blink of an eye. He sat down on the bed and pulled her very gently into his arms and held her as close as he dared while she cried.

Seven

"**I** didn't mean to make it sound as if you were a burden," he said at her temple. His dark, lean hand gently stroked her hair away from her pale face.

Her fist clenched against his chest. "I don't want to stay here," she sobbed.

His eyes, unseen above her head, were tormented. "Yes. I know."

"Please," she whispered. "Brad can...look in on me."

"You can't be alone. Brad has to work," he said tersely. "It wouldn't be proper for him to take care of you."

"It isn't proper for me to stay here, either!"

"It will be, when the nurse arrives," he said coolly. He eased her away from him and against the pillows. He took a tissue from the box at the bedside and softly dabbed it against her red eyes. She looked utterly defeated, worn to the bone. She was far too thin and pale and he didn't like her color.

"I'm going to bring supper home with me," he said. "And you're going to eat it. You can't continue like this."

"I don't want food," she said.

"You'll eat, even if I have to feed you every bite," he replied tersely.

She looked at him with red, tormented eyes. Every bit of her ordeal was in that drawn face, in those gray eyes.

His fingers spread against her cool, wet cheek in a caress. Her vulnerability made him feel protective. "I'll take care of you," he said softly. "Try to sleep." He bent and, to her astonishment, drew his lips tenderly over her mouth. "I'll be home as soon as I can."

He stood up, searching her face for some reaction. She looked shocked.

"Do you need anything before I go?"

She shook her head, idly stroking the kitten while she tried to decide what his motive was for that unexpected caress.

"Stay in bed. I'll help you walk, or the nurse will."

She nodded, averting her eyes.

His chin lifted and he stared down at her with faint arrogance. "Don't you want to ask why I kissed you?"

The color rushed into her cheeks. She couldn't bear to lift her eyes. Her fingers clenched in the coverlet.

He could almost feel her discomfort. It was too soon for this, he thought, surprised at his own behavior. He hadn't meant to upset her. God knew, she'd been through enough.

"Try to get some more sleep," he said, his voice formal now, almost professional.

She managed a nod.

He paused to ruffle the kitten's soft fur. "I call her Mosquito," he said. "She's always buzzing around. You'd better think of a proper name."

She didn't answer. His fingers slid from the kitten to her clenched hand. He pressed it gently.

"I'm sorry," he said softly. "I didn't mean to make you ill at ease. I'll see you later."

He turned and went out, leaving the bedroom door open. She heard him on the telephone, but she was tired and sleepy. Before he left the apartment, she was already dozing.

Nurse Plimm came back that afternoon. More aware now than she'd been those first days out of surgery, Noreen realized that Polly Plimm was in her fifties, a cozy, kind woman with the comportment of a drill sergeant. She took over the apartment at once. When Ramon came in with a box of prepared food, she got out plates and made coffee and poured more fruit juice. She stood over Noreen until the younger woman gave in and lifted a forkful of grilled chicken to her reluctant mouth.

"There, isn't that delicious?" she asked. "Now you eat while I sort out your medicines."

The minute she was gone, Noreen put the fork down, staring blankly at the delicate fruit compote and the braised asparagus and the delicious home-made roll on her plate. She wasn't hungry. How was she going to manage to eat all that? She felt as if she were an interloper in Ramon's apartment, even if it wasn't the one he'd shared with his beloved Isadora.

Having Noreen here would surely be like a repeat of a nightmare to him. She wanted so badly to go back to her apartment, but he wouldn't let her.

"Not eating?" he chided softly from the doorway. He'd taken off his jacket and tie. His shirtsleeves were rolled up and his white shirt was unbuttoned at the neck. Even disheveled, he looked elegant and far too sensuous.

"I'm trying," she said defensively, her eyes on her plate.

He moved into the room, sitting down gently on the bed beside her. He took the fork from her listless fingers and speared a cube of fruit, taking it to her lips.

"Don't..." she protested.

He eased the fruit past her parted lips, moving it softly against the tender skin with a pressure that was frankly seductive. She must surely be imagining that, she told herself, as she glanced upward.

His eyes were dark, half-closed as he looked down at her. He was so handsome, she thought miserably. She'd never seen a man so sensuous and desirable in her life, and she had to look like a comedy hour reject.

He leaned closer, his eyes falling to her soft mouth. "Eat it," he breathed, teasing her lips again.

She opened them involuntarily, accepting the bit of fruit, hardly tasting it as she chewed.

His gaze slid down to the scar that showed above the white cotton gown the nurse had helped her don. Her heartbeat was shaking her, but it was regular and quick, with the telltale mechanical chinking sound of the new valve as it opened and closed in her heart.

"Is the pain easier?" he asked. "You have capsules for that, if you need them."

"It's only sore," she began.

"Here?" His long finger traced the edge of the scar down into the gown, and she gasped and caught his strong wrist.

He smiled, as if her sudden flush delighted him. He moved his hand to the pillow beside her head and busied himself with another forkful of food from her plate.

"You can't..." she protested in a whisper.

"Yes, I can." He fed her, slowly, sensuously, watching her mouth as she accepted one bite after another and swallowed it. His level gaze made her heart race. He saw it, and heard it, and she hated her traitorous body for being so vulnerable.

Ramon was delighted. She wasn't indifferent to him, at least. That meant that he might be able to make amends for the pain he'd dealt her. He wasn't certain yet of his motives, but he liked the way she reacted to him. Her vulnerability fed his pride, made him arrogant with pleasure. It had been a long time since he'd felt so alive, so much a man.

The entrance of Miss Plimm interrupted his introspective thoughts. He smiled at her.

"Time for medicine," the older woman said with a smile. She handed the paper cup to Ramon. "Nice to have your own doctor so close at hand, hmmm?" she teased as she went away.

Ramon tipped the pills into her mouth and handed her the fruit juice, his strong arm propping her up so that she could swallow. In the position, the gown was loose, all but baring her firm, pretty breasts. She saw

Ramon's eyes drop to study them and she sat back quickly, blushing.

His eyes met hers. "I'm a doctor," he reminded her.

She averted her gaze to her fruit juice and didn't answer.

She heard the soft sigh that passed his lips as he got up from the bed and stood beside it thoughtfully, with his hands in his pockets.

"Finish your supper," he said quietly. "I'll be back in to check on you later. I have some paperwork to get through in the study."

She nodded without looking at him. Her heart was all but beating her to death, and it wasn't because of the artificial valve. She hated being this way, and having him see it.

He read that resentment in her face, but he was at a loss for words. She'd seemed attracted to him before the surgery, but now her only thought seemed to be to keep him at arm's length.

He began to think back over the years. Flashes of memory imprinted in his mind. Noreen, much younger, blushing when he looked at her, hiding from him, watching him with eyes that fell the instant he saw her. Dressing in shapeless clothes. Backing away.

He scowled, puzzled. It had been like that since he'd first come home with Isadora. Isadora was beautiful, of course. Her very presence had kept his attention from wandering to the pale shadow that Noreen had been. But now the past seemed so vivid and real. Noreen had never visited her cousin after she married Ramon. She'd avoided him, even at work, arranging her shifts so that they rarely coincided with his.

He felt unsettled. He didn't like thinking back. It

was disconcerting. He'd never permitted himself to really look at Noreen, or to wonder why he cut at her so often. He'd spent years deliberately antagonizing her.

He put the memories away and left Noreen to her supper. For the rest of the evening he was so quiet that his return to check his patient at bedtime startled both women. He did a cursory examination, pronounced Noreen improving, asked Miss Plimm to fetch the pain capsules and went to bed, still remote and distracted.

It irritated him more than he liked to admit when Brad came to the door that Saturday with a bouquet of flowers for Noreen. He admitted the man to the apartment, letting Miss Plimm usher him into the bedroom.

He hadn't thought of flowers. It was obvious that Noreen was touched and surprised at Brad's gesture. Ramon hadn't given her so much as a dandelion, and he felt the omission keenly as he watched the younger man bend to kiss Noreen's pale cheek and saw the sudden warm smile on her lips for the man.

He went back into his study and closed the door firmly. Noreen's love life was none of his business, he told himself. Her physical reaction to him was a fluke, only a cruel twist of fate. She didn't like him. She might be vulnerable physically, but she fought that with everything in her, now more than ever.

He'd made sure that he never gave her any reason to like him. He'd been sarcastic to her during his marriage and viciously hateful toward her after Isadora's untimely death. He'd been a stranger to her, deliberately.

He stared at the portrait of Isadora on the wall, the one she'd demanded to have done by a famous portrait artist just after their marriage. The eyes, china blue, were as empty of feeling as the wall. The artist had truly captured the essence of Isadora, beautiful and shallow. Ironically she'd loved the rendering.

He poured himself a drink, since he wasn't on call for once, and sat down in the chair to sip it. Seconds later, the kitten scampered across the carpet and vaulted into his lap, to curl close and purr.

He petted it indulgently, watching the huge green eyes look up at him worshipfully. At least, he thought, the cat liked him.

Miss Plimm came into the room with a glance at the bedroom, from which pleasant laughter issued.

"Shall I ask the cook to put supper back half an hour, sir?" she asked softly.

He sighed. "You might as well. They sound as if they've got a lot to talk about."

"You look so tired, sir," she said. "Isn't there something I can bring you?"

He lifted his glass. "I have all I need, thanks."

She glanced toward the bedroom. "Dozens of blooms," she muttered, "and her just out of the hospital. Clog her lungs up, they will, but people never think, do they?"

She wandered back toward her own room and Ramon glanced back toward the bedroom. Strange that the thought of Isadora's lover hadn't bothered him half as much as Noreen's friend did. He leaned back in the chair and closed his eyes.

It was an hour later that Miss Plimm gently shook him.

"A call?" he asked, blinking as he came immediately awake.

"No, sir, supper," she said. "Mr. Donaldson's gone home."

"Oh."

She had the bouquet of flowers in her hand. "I'm just going to put these in the dining room," she said.

"Doesn't she mind?" he asked coolly.

She frowned at him. "I didn't ask, sir." She moved away with her burden.

He went to the bedroom and looked inside. She wasn't in the bed. He heard the bathroom door open and saw her come slowly out of it, breathless.

"Couldn't you call for help?" he muttered.

Before she could say a word, he scooped her up and carried her back to bed.

Her stiffness conducted itself right through his jacket. He looked down at her, poised beside the bed, and frowned at the expression in her eyes.

"You're frightened," he said at once, and his eyes narrowed again. "Why?"

She swallowed. "Put me down…"

He ignored the nervous request. He was thinking, his gaze reflective and steady. "Shapeless clothes," he murmured, "no makeup, always backing away. Why?"

"You have no right," she began.

"But you'll tell me anyway."

"I will not," she asserted.

He sat down on the edge of the bed with Noreen across his lap. He shifted her against his shoulder and his free hand rested against the silky gown, just under her breast.

Her hand had gone to his strong wrist and caught

there, pleading. But he didn't move. His fingers began to spread, very tenderly. And all the time, he watched her face with calculating eyes.

She gasped as his forefinger gently spread against the hard nipple, just enough to make her shiver. Her hand lost its will on his wrist and relaxed. She moaned.

"Querida," he breathed, and without thought for where they were, for the open door, the past, he pulled the gown down away from her shoulder and his lips pressed tenderly on the soft, warm flesh of her breast that the action exposed.

"Ramon," she whispered, sobbing as her hands tangled in his black hair, struggling for control that was utterly lost the moment he touched her skin. "Oh…dear Lord…don't!"

But while her hoarse voice pleaded, her traitorous body arched itself painfully, trying to get closer to his warm mouth and she shuddered with the pleasure his lips gave her body.

She felt his hands on her, gently moving, guiding her down to the bed, to the pillow, while his mouth fed on her. He could feel her breathing under his lips, hear the frantic rush of her heartbeat. His own body was taut, and so hungry that he ached from his head to his toes.

The sound of plates on wood lifted his head. He looked down at the softness of Noreen's pretty breast where his mouth had pressed so hungrily, past the thin red scar down her breastbone and up the creamy expanse of skin to her wide, shocked eyes.

She caught at her gown, but his hand stayed it. He looked down at her breast again, fascinated by its

firm, soft contours, the creamy blush of it in the stillness of the room.

"The cook's ready to put the food on the table,
Doctor!" Miss Plimm called from a room away.

Ramon could hardly breathe normally. His eyes
met Noreen's, steady and relentless as he saw and felt
and heard her helpless response to him.

He looked down at her once more, his eyes hungry
for her nudity. With a groan, he managed to cover
her and stand up, with his back to the bed and the
door, apparently staring out the window while he
fought the demons of desire that tore at his body. It
had been years...

Footsteps came closer. "Doctor?" Miss Plimm
called.

"I'll be right there," he said curtly.

"Yes, sir. Can I bring you anything, Miss Kensington?"

"No, thank you," Noreen managed to say calmly.

"Well, if you need anything, just you call!"

"Yes, Miss Plimm, thank you," she replied.

Her body throbbed from head to toe. She couldn't
even look at Ramon. She was ashamed of her help-
lessness, her impotence.

After a minute, he moved back to the bed, and the
flash of desire in his eyes made her shiver.

She clutched the sheet close, in pain again from the
movement of her body and showing it.

Without a word, he opened the bottle of pain capsules and, holding her hand palm up, shook two into
it. He guided it to her lips and then held a glass of
water to help her swallow it.

He put the glass away, pulling the cover back up

to her waist. His dark, turbulent eyes met her embarrassed ones.

He brushed back a few wispy strands of her hair, his expression grim. His head bent and he brushed a kiss against her forehead.

She tried to speak, but his lean fingers over her mouth stilled the words.

"There are in life a few moments so beautiful," he whispered, "that even words are a sort of profanity."

She caught her breath at the look in his eyes, even though what he was saying didn't seem to make sense.

"Go to sleep," he said gently.

Amazingly her eyes closed, still full of him, her body taut with unfamiliar needs and wants that she had no idea how to fulfill. The pain and shock and weariness slowly took their toll on her. Shortly thereafter, she fell into a deep and profound sleep.

She pretended stubbornly that nothing had happened. But Ramon knew everything he needed to know about her earlier behavior now. The old clothes, the camouflage—it wasn't because of some dreadful childhood experience, as he'd first suspected. It was to keep him from knowing how easily he affected her, how desperately vulnerable she was to him. The instant he touched her, her body belonged to him. Now he knew it. And she knew, too.

There was a sort of affectionate arrogance in the way he looked at her, as if he'd already possessed her, and knew every inch of her under her clothing. He wasn't blatant about it, but he knew. She became more uneasy as the days passed, afraid that he was going to do something about it. She was also having more discomfort than ever, soreness and pain in the breastbone, and she couldn't sleep without pain medication. It was a comfort to have Nurse Plimm nearby, not only because she knew what to do when Noreen was in pain, but also because she made a nice buffer between Noreen and Ramon. Despite his tenderness of recent days, Noreen didn't trust him an inch.

Certainly he was sorry that he'd misjudged her reason for leaving Isadora alone, but his grief at his beloved wife's loss had been very real. And regardless of the contributing factors, Noreen's absence had been the ultimate cause of Isadora's death, even if she couldn't help doing it. Ramon had loved Isadora obsessively. That grief and anger wouldn't vanish in a haze just because Noreen had heart surgery. This was only the calm before the storm. When she was well again, she had little doubt that Ramon would return to his usual, vengeful self, and she wasn't giving him any openings. Weaknesses were dangerous. If she let him see how attracted she was to him, might he not use that attraction to his advantage to avenge the loss of Isadora?

These thoughts and fears led to a withdrawing of herself when Ramon was around, to a visible remoteness and formality. Ramon seemed to expect it. At least, he didn't try to circumvent it.

Meanwhile, Ramon worked himself to the point of exhaustion to keep the memories of Noreen in his arms at bay. She was weak and all too vulnerable in her present condition, and a guest in his house. He had no right whatsoever to take advantage of it.

The problem, he mused grimly, was that his feelings for her had been so forcefully repressed over the years that he had to fight now to keep them under control. Not until Noreen's sudden, shocking illness had he really faced what he felt. Even now, it was hard to admit it, if just in the privacy of his own thoughts.

It hadn't taken two months of marriage to Isadora to know that he'd made a mistake. But his honor and pride had forced him to make the best of a relationship sanctioned by the Church. Tradition had chained him to his vows. No one had ever known his true feelings, because he'd hidden them so well. He professed lifelong devotion to Isadora, showed the world a true love surpassing the most romantic expectations. But behind the smiles and lies was a cold, lifeless marriage between two totally unsuited people. Isadora's beauty had blinded him to her true nature, which was exactly the opposite of Noreen's.

He sipped coffee with a weariness that was unlike him during an all-too-brief break between surgeries, sitting in the hospital cafeteria. Isadora's death had made him realize how barren their marriage had been. His own guilt about leaving her so often alone had assumed massive proportions then, and it had been convenient to blame Noreen for deserting her cousin. His guilt had fed that blame. Noreen had paid a very high price for Isadora's death. Now it seemed so futile and heartless, to have heaped such cruelties on the head of a sick woman who could easily have died herself that very night.

The Kensingtons were obviously feeling some of the same guilt that he felt over Noreen. He'd had a call from her uncle at his office, which he had yet to return. Noreen hadn't professed any desire to see her aunt and uncle since she'd been released from the hospital, and their request to come and visit her had been turned down abruptly and without explanation. They, like Ramon, wanted to start again. Noreen very obviously didn't.

He finished his coffee and stretched. He wondered exactly how Noreen felt about her friend Brad, who felt comfortable bringing her flowers and sitting with her by the hour. He didn't like the man, and for no logical reason. To admit the cause was jealousy was more than he could bring himself to do.

With a long sigh, he glanced at his watch and grimaced. Back to work, he thought, and was grateful that he had something to occupy his mind. Lately his thoughts were poor companions indeed.

It was a surprise to find the Kensingtons waiting at his office when he finished at the hospital. They'd made an appointment, at that.

Noreen's uncle was the first to speak, after they were seated in Ramon's spartan but luxurious office.

"We want to know what we can do for her," he told Ramon without preamble.

"Yes," Mary added quietly. "There must be something—the hospital bill, therapy, her lost salary—"

"She won't talk to us," her uncle continued, interrupting his wife in his haste to get the words out. "But we don't blame her for that, you know. We just want to help. We've been very much at fault," he added uneasily.

"So have I," Ramon replied grimly. "All of us so easily put the blame on her. She had a mild heart attack that night, or so her physician thinks," he continued, having told them this before, but uncertain if they remembered. "He sedated her while she was still trying to make him understand about the condition Isadora was in.'' He folded his hands on the desk and stared at its highly polished surface. ''She feels guilty even about that, and none of us considered her own feelings in the matter. She cared about Isadora, too. She wasn't allowed to go to the funeral, to be part of the family—even to grieve.''

Mary bit her lower lip to stop the tears, and they were genuine ones. She'd loved her daughter so much that she'd pushed her niece cruelly aside. It hadn't been easy to look back down the long years and see how all of them, especially Isadora, had made such good use of Noreen without caring about her own wishes or hopes. She'd been neglected shamefully, even her health.

''We didn't know she had a heart condition,'' Mary murmured. ''We never even bothered to make sure she had a physical before she started college.''

''We didn't care,'' Hal said shortly, his face full of self-contempt. ''We never cared. She bought me an eel skin wallet for my birthday this year, you remember, Ramon. It must have cost her a week's salary and I couldn't even resist making a joke of that.'' He put his head in his hands with a weary sigh. ''I feel sick. Just sick. You know, she accused us of coming to see her to stop people from gossiping, and I guess that's how she feels.'' He looked up. ''But it wasn't that. We were genuinely shocked and sorry about what happened to her. We want to see her. Can't you do something? Talk to her, plead our case? At least, we could help her financially if she needs it.''

Ramon stared at them for a moment. ''Let me think about it for a few days,'' he said solemnly. ''I'll try to find a way. Hopefully, one for all of us.''

Eight

But if thinking about a way to approach Noreen was easy, putting the thought into action wasn't. Since Ramon had kissed her, she'd withdrawn into a very thick shell. Miss Plimm noticed Noreen's sudden shyness and apprehension about Ramon, and she'd spoken to him one evening.

"At her age, despite the weakness and pain, she should be picking up better than this," Nurse Plimm said bluntly. "She's very much on edge. I've noticed that it accelerates when you're around her."

He sat down in his burgundy leather recliner and leaned back, weary from a long day at the operating table.

"I've noticed it, too," he replied quietly, motioning her to a seat on the black leather couch across from him. "You're aware that Noreen and I have had our misunderstandings over the years?'' he asked with keen eyes on her face.

She folded her arms. ''She said that.''

''It was mostly my fault, for accepting that she left my wife alone in a critical condition and permitted her to die.'' He held up his hand when she started to speak. ''Please, let me finish. I know now that Noreen was in no way to blame for what happened. I have been very much in the wrong, as have her aunt and uncle, and we acknowledge this. But Noreen has become so remote that we find it impossible to approach her.'' He spread his hands. ''We've reached an impasse. None of us knows what to do. I don't blame her for the way she feels, you understand. But we want to make our peace. And she won't let us.''

''She's still in a good deal of pain,'' Nurse Plimm replied, ''and you know, yourself, sir, that a period of confusion often follows such radical surgery.''

''I know it,'' he agreed. ''It's just that I've never experienced it on such a personal basis.''

''She needs time to adjust,'' she continued. ''That's all. Be patient.''

''That isn't one of my better qualities, I'm afraid, except in surgery,'' he replied with a faint smile. ''But I'll try.''

She got up from her chair. ''And by the way, sir, I've told Mr. Donaldson not to bring any more flowers,'' she added. ''It isn't healthy, especially not just after surgery. He should know that.''

His eyes narrowed. ''He's been back recently to see her?''

Now she really looked uncomfortable. ''He comes every other afternoon, sir,'' she replied. ''I thought you knew.''

He dismissed her and sat brooding, with eyes like black steel in a drawn face. No, he hadn't known about Brad's visits. It angered him that the man kept coming here. Noreen was his business now, not Donaldson's. Well, he'd arrange to be at home the next time Noreen's caller arrived, and he'd put the man straight about visiting!

It never once occurred to him that he was being unreasonable. Not until he opened the door to Donaldson the following Friday and told him that Noreen wasn't up to so many visits just yet.

"Why?" Donaldson asked shortly.

The older man just stared at him. He was actually speechless, because there wasn't really a good reason for his objection to Donaldson's visits.

"I'm careful not to tire her," Donaldson continued, trying to placate Ramon, who looked formidable with his black eyes flashing. "I know how frail she is."

Frail. Yes, she was frail, Ramon thought, almost fragile. She'd been that way for a long time, but her independence and spirit had blinded him to it.

He leaned against the door frame wearily. "She's not healing as quickly as I expected her to," he said after a minute. "She doesn't sleep at night, despite the pain medication, and she's constantly restless."

Donaldson's chin lifted. "Perhaps it's the environment," he said, and added, "not that you can help the way you feel, sir, I realize that. But even hidden hostility certainly doesn't help. She's tense all the time now."

That was a blow, but Ramon had the grace to accept it without exploding. He'd been hostile to Noreen for so long that everyone around him knew how he'd felt about her. Now, he'd installed her in his apartment and he expected her to warm to him immediately. In fact, he was resentful because she hadn't. He must have been out of his mind to expect so much, despite the fact that she'd melted in his arms. Even that might have seemed like a threat to her, an underhanded way to play on her vulnerability and hurt her. He wouldn't do that now, but she wouldn't know it. He was the biggest obstacle in her recovery. Amazing, he thought, that it had taken an outsider to point the fact out to him.

He stood aside. "Talk to her," he said unexpectedly. "See if she'd rather go back to her apartment. Miss Plimm can go with her, and she'll have any other help she needs."

"That's decent of you, sir," Donaldson said, surprised.

Ramon's dark eyebrows arched expressively. "Have I shocked you, Donaldson?"

The younger man shifted nervously. "Everyone knows how much you dislike Noreen."

He nodded toward Noreen's bedroom and went back to his study, closing the door quietly. But he was far too preoccupied to do any work.

Brad grinned around the door at Noreen, who brightened a little when she saw him.

"Down in the dumps again?" he teased, closing the door until it was barely cracked. His expression cleared at once. He sat down beside her on the bed. "Dr. Cortero just said that if you want to, you can go back to your apartment now. He'll send Miss Plimm with you, and you can have any help you need."

Her breath escaped in a rush. It was a relief. Such

a relief. Being near Ramon was torture. "When?" she asked immediately.

"As soon as you like, I gather. He told me to mention it to you." He touched her hair gently. "You don't like it here, do you?"

She shook her head, lowering her eyes to his chin. "He's been very kind," she said, "but I'd like to be at home, with familiar things around me. I'm sure that I get in his way, even though he's careful not to let it show. He can't even have…people…in while I'm lying around."

"People?"

She shrugged. "Women," she murmured.

"That would be one for the books," he replied. "Not even the notorious grapevine can find one single bit of gossip about him. He doesn't go out with anyone. I suppose he's still mourning his wife."

"Yes," she said, and the thought hurt. "He was obsessed with Isadora. They had to drag him away from the coffin at the graveside service." She didn't like remembering that.

"He must have loved her very much."

"More than his life. That's why he hates me so much. I suppose he's not as judgmental as he was, not since this happened to me. But the fact is, he left me in charge of her welfare and I let her die." Her eyes were haunted as she looked up at him. "I loved her, too," she said gruffly. "Even if none of them thought so. She could be kind, when she wanted to. She couldn't help the way she was. Everyone spoiled her because she was so pretty—even me."

"Beauty is skin deep," he said coolly. "It doesn't have a thing to do with a person's character. I'd take you, any day, if I were free."

She smiled gently. "Thanks."

He patted her hand. "You never date, either," he murmured. "Are you eating your heart out, figuratively speaking, for someone you can't have, too?"

She didn't want to answer that. She had to harden her resolve. Ramon was willing to let her leave, so apparently he was getting tired of her presence in the apartment. It must be torment to him, a constant reminder of Isadora. She refused to dwell on those kisses. Probably he'd been lonely so long that any female, in whatever condition, would have evoked the same response from him.

She lay back against the pillows. She'd have to let Miss Plimm come with her, and somehow she'd have to manage her salary. But she would.

"Ask him," she said finally, "when I can leave."

Ramon's face didn't betray a single trace of emotion when Brad put the question to him.

"I'll make the arrangements," he said, showing Brad to the door. "I'll tell her. The sooner the better."

Brad nodded. "Thanks. I really believe she'll get back on her feet sooner if she's in familiar surroundings. No matter how cushy someone else's place is, it's never home."

"So I see." Ramon closed the door behind Brad and hesitated before he went into Noreen's bedroom. She was sitting very stiffly against the pillows, her hands folded tightly in her lap. Miss Plimm had gone out to lunch and was taking a few hours off afterward to do her banking and shopping, since it was Friday.

"You can go in the morning if you like," he told her without preamble. "I'll speak to Miss Plimm when she returns. There's just one thing," he added, nodding toward the kitten curled up at her feet on the coverlet. "You can't take Mosquito with you."

"I know that," she said sadly. She'd grown attached to the tiny thing. But rules were rules, and she couldn't hide the cat if the owner and his wife were coming in and out of the apartment—which they would, being the kind of people who did whatever they could for the sick.

"I'll take good care of her," Ramon added.

She nodded.

He made an irritated sound. "Look here, why don't you want to stay? You've got everything you need at hand. Donaldson visits all the time. Why are you so anxious to go home to that lonely apartment?"

She looked up at him with a drawn, weary face. "Because it's mine," she said. "It's all I have."

He felt that right down to his shoes. "What do you mean?"

"I mean that I live alone," she said. "I like living alone. I'm uncomfortable around people."

"Around me, you mean."

Her jaw tautened. "Yes."

He moved closer to the bed. His dark eyes probed her face. "I make you uncomfortable."

Her eyes darted away. Her heart was racing wildly, betraying her excitement.

"Talk to me," he said sharply.

Her hands gripped each other as if her life depended on it. She clenched her teeth. She wouldn't look at him at all.

He rammed his hands into his pockets to keep from grabbing her. As always, she aroused fierce emotions in him. But now he was less armored against them than usual.

"It isn't that I don't appreciate all you've done for me," she said after a minute. "I'm very grateful. You saved my life. You certainly didn't have to sacrifice your privacy on my behalf, as well."

"My privacy, as you put it, is a very lonely one," he said, surprising her into looking up at his lean, handsome face. "I don't entertain. I thought you knew."

"But...you always used to," she began.

"When Isadora was alive," he agreed. He searched her drawn face quietly. "Isadora had parties. She couldn't live unless she was surrounded by people and music. I spent more and more time at my office, because I never had the solitude to review my medical journals or prepare papers here. She resented my work, almost from the beginning of our lives together. She wanted me to give it up, did you know?"

She shook her head. "It would have been a pity if you had," she said. "You're the best in your field. Didn't she know how many lives you've saved?"

"She didn't care," he said simply. "Isadora's only real interest was Isadora. That's what happens to many spoiled children. They grow up with no compassion for others, only concerned with their wants, their needs. Then they marry and have families and they aren't equipped to deal with the self-sacrifice. Eventually, they fall apart. Just as Isadora did."

"She always seemed very happy," she told him. "So did you."

"Oh, one puts on a public face, so as not to admit one's failings," he mused. "We were the picture of the ideal happy couple, yes? And underneath was Isadora's jealousy and discontent, and growing dependence on alcohol and parties to get her through the long, lonely days and nights.''

He'd never spoken in such a way. She gaped at him, totally without the capacity to interrupt.

''It wasn't enough for her to love. She had to own. Possess. But she was cold inside. She had nothing to give except her beauty and the shallow affection behind it.'' He sighed, staring at Noreen quietly. ''In bed, she was the coldest human being I ever knew. She only wanted it over with, and she was obsessed with contraception.''

''But she said that you didn't want children,'' she blurted out.

''I wanted them, all right.''

She knew what he meant, suddenly, instinctively. There was something in his passionate nature that adored children, wanted them, valued them. But she hadn't known, because Ramon had never spoken of these things to her before.

''I've gone hungry for a woman's passion,'' he said gently. ''I've been starved of it. That's why I lost control with you. The novelty of a woman's willing mouth and clinging arms was almost too much for me. I'd never known it, you see. Isadora wanted my fame and my wealth and my name. But she never wanted me.''

''She adored you,'' she protested.

''She adored my money,'' he said with a cynical laugh. ''And what it could buy her. Do you know, she'd had a lover before me? And she didn't give him up, just because she was married. She had the same lover when she died. She wanted to go to Paris with me because she knew he was going to be there. She warned me that if I made her stay at home, she'd do something to get even with me.'' His eyes were full of bitterness as he spoke of it. ''She did, too. She got even in the basest way she could. She died, and left me with the guilt of responsibility for it.''

''You blamed me,'' she began.

''I blamed myself,'' he said angrily. ''I still do. Blaming you was the only way I could live with it, for a long time.'' He searched her face with dark, solemn eyes. ''As if you could let anyone or anything die,'' he scoffed, ''with that tenderness in you that makes me curse myself for all the harsh words and accusations I've thrown at you in the past.'' He drew in a harsh breath. ''You did nothing except show me what Isadora was. Worse, you showed me what she wasn't.''

''I don't understand.''

''How could you?'' he asked grimly. ''You don't know me. I couldn't let you know me, because it was dangerous for us to be close to each other.''

Her eyes were frankly puzzled.

''You don't understand?'' he asked with soft amusement.

''No,'' she said honestly.

He moved slowly to the bed and sat down beside her. His lean hand went to her lips and he traced them softly, his gaze holding hers until her heartbeat erupted into a frenzy of excitement.

''Now, do you understand?'' he asked in the merest whisper. ''Here. Feel.''

He brought her hand to his chest and pressed her fingers, palm down, to his heart. It was beating wildly, just like her own. In his dark eyes, she could see the same turbulence she was feeling. But as she looked up into the face she loved most in all the world, she saw only desire. He wanted her, yes. But it wasn't a desire that rose out of love. It was a physical trick of the senses. Just that.

She let her hand fall back to the coverlet with a soft sigh. "I see."

"I don't think you do," he replied grimly. "You're afraid to let yourself see it." He put a finger over lips that tried to form words. "I know that you're attracted to me, Noreen, and you don't want to be. I've worked too hard at making you hate me over the years."

That was funny, but she wasn't laughing. He really had no idea how she felt about him. He thought she only wanted him. Her gaze fell to keep him from seeing what was in them, and she drew back against the pillows, defensively.

He mistook the action for fear and got to his feet. "It's all right," he said quietly. "I won't make any blatant passes. Everyone seems to feel that I'm the reason you aren't improving rapidly enough. If you want to go back to your apartment, I'll send you there. You can have anything you want to make you more comfortable. Well, anything except Mosquito," he murmured, smiling faintly as the kitten stretched and rolled onto its back.

She noticed the way he looked at the tiny thing, and her heart ached for the children he didn't have, the animals Isadora had refused to have in the apartment.

He looked up and caught that expression in her eyes. He was surprised and delighted by it. "Are you feeling sorry for me, *¿querida?*" he asked gently.

"Quizás un poco," she murmured in Spanish. *Perhaps, a little.*

He moved closer to the bed. "Your accent is flawless," he said softly. "Do you understand it as well as you speak it?"

"Sometimes," she admitted, "but it depends on the speaker. I understand a Cuban accent best, because my Spanish professor was from Havana."

"We tend to drop the *'s'* in words or run over it," he mused. "So you can understand me when I speak Spanish," he added calculatingly. His lips pursed. "Then, if you stayed here, until you're well enough to take care of yourself, I could read Baroja to you in the evenings."

She bunched the bedspread under her hands. "Isadora gave you a copy of *Paradox, Rey,*" she recalled.

"Which you picked out for her," he replied, surprising her, "because Isadora never spoke one word of Spanish. She thought it a boring language, and she had nothing but contempt for Spanish authors like Baroja."

"He was one of my favorites," she admitted. "He was a renegade, but he knew so much about suffering and poverty. He knew people inside out."

"Of course. He was a doctor before he was a novelist." He smiled. "Do you like Zorrilla?"

She smiled. *"Don Juan Tenorio,"* she quoted.

"How appropriate that you should remember that particular work," he murmured, smiling faintly. "Unlike the Don Juan who was damned in Tirso de Molina's version of the story, Zorrilla's Don Juan was saved from hell by the love of a good woman."

"Yes. It was a wonderful story." She moved her shoulders and lay back against the pillows with a long sigh, wincing because she was still having some discomfort. Her hand went to the scar.

"You won't have much of a scar when it heals," he remarked, watching her touch the incision. "I pride myself on my stitching."

She smiled. "You do it very well." Her gaze lifted to his. "You've been very kind to me."

"And you think that kindness was prompted by a guilty conscience?"

"The thought had crossed my mind."

His hands moved in his pockets. "Well, it isn't altogether guilt. Not anymore, at least." He looked at her quietly. "I like taking care of you, isn't that strange?" he mused. "I've never really had anyone to come home to before, much less someone of my own who needed tending to." His mouth twisted. "I've gotten...used to having you here." The smile faded. "You'll hate your apartment," he said abruptly. "Even with Miss Plimm for company."

"You think that your company is so indispensable?" she asked irritably.

"Perhaps it is, Noreen," he said, his voice deep and somber. "I don't think you quite realize how accustomed you've become to my routine. You fit in here."

Her heart raced again. She felt hemmed in, imprisoned. Yet he hadn't taken even a step toward her.

"Stay," he said roughly.

She was flustered. She couldn't get her mind to work at all. "I'm in the way," she faltered. "And Brad comes, and you don't like him here..."

"I can tolerate your friend," he said shortly. "You don't get in the way."

She hesitated. She didn't want to stay, but she

didn't want to leave. It was a risk, being near him. He didn't know yet how she really felt about him, but if she stayed here long enough, he would. On the other hand, she'd had a tremendous scare about her heart. It was comforting to her to have him close at hand, for professional as well as personal reasons. Too, there was Mosquito. She'd miss the kitten. She had exquisite meals, prepared by his daily cook. The room was nice…

Her rationalizing irritated her, and she glared at him for putting the temptation in her path.

He only smiled. "Stay," he coaxed. "I'll read to you every night."

"Baroja?" she asked softly.

"Whatever you like," he said huskily.

She could imagine that deep, velvety voice reading Spanish poetry in a lamplit room, and she blushed.

"Nothing sensuous," he teased. "We want your heart beating nicely, not galloping. Not just yet, anyway."

She was already lost. "If I'm really not in the way…"

The kitten came stretching and yawning up to her shoulder and curled up against her neck. Her hair, in its bun, began to escape with Mosquito's restless movements.

"Your hair needs washing," he remarked. "Miss Plimm can do it for you tomorrow, if you feel up to it." His eyes narrowed. "Do you ever let it down?" he asked.

"Not very much," she confessed. "It gets in the way at work, and when I try to sleep, it gets in my eyes and mouth. I thought about getting it cut, but I love long hair."

"So do I," he said. He stared at her for a moment, picturing that wealth of hair in his hands, against his bare chest...

He turned abruptly, catching his breath. "I'll tell Miss Plimm to stop packing."

There were so many things she wanted to ask him, to tell him, but nothing came to mind at all. She closed her eyes. How suddenly living with Ramon had become a way of life. She hadn't really wanted to leave. For whatever reasons of his own, he seemed to feel the same way. Only time would tell if she'd made the right decision.

"There's one other thing," he said from the open doorway.

"Yes?"

"Your aunt and uncle would very much like to come and see you," he said, watching her face tighten. "I know how you must feel about them, but in their way, they're sorry and they want to make amends."

She looked up at him helplessly, her mind full of the long years without love, without tenderness. It was there in her big gray eyes, an open wound.

Ramon went back to her and sat down on the bed, grasping one of her hands and holding it firmly in his big, warm one. "Forgiveness is never easy, Noreen," he said. "But without it, wars would never end. We all have to stop living in the past and start again." He searched those sad eyes. "Let it start here, with us. Can you forgive me?"

She felt his hand contract around her fingers. "Of course," she said, not able to meet his eyes. "I never really blamed you for the way you felt."

"You never knew how I felt, Noreen," he said quietly.

She lifted her gaze to his and searched the dark softness of his eyes. "Everyone knew. You hated me."

He shook his head. "I only tried to. It never really worked." His eyes narrowed as if in pain. "Have you ever heard the saying that sorrow carves a deep place in us to hold the happiness that comes afterward? Perhaps it will be like that for you. I hope so. It would please me to see you happy. It would please your aunt and uncle, too. Don't push us away."

He was a powerful advocate. She closed her eyes and grimaced at the discomfort where the stitches were. "All right," she said after a minute. "I'll try, if they will."

He lifted her hand to his mouth, turned it and kissed the palm with breathless tenderness. She actually flushed at the action.

He smiled as he gave her hand back to her. "I have some reading to do and then I have to make rounds. But tomorrow night, if you like, I'll read to you."

Her heart jumped at just the thought. She smiled back, fascinated by this complex man. "I would like it."

He got up from the bed and studied her with amused indulgence. "So would I. I'll check on you later."

She watched him leave the room and felt as if her life had just taken a sixty-degree turn. Her only real concern was his motive. He felt an attraction to her, he felt sorry for her, she knew that. But there was something else in his eyes lately when he looked at her. And there was the exquisite, tender care he took

of her. She could never remember seeing him so careful of Isadora's comfort, not even in the early weeks
of their marriage. All of these things together formed
a puzzle she couldn't quite solve. But being in the
cocoon he made for her was so sweet that she
couldn't force herself to give it up. Not just yet.

Before he went to bed that night, he paused in the
doorway of her room and stood just looking at her
for a long moment.

"Will you want to go back to work, when you're
well again?" he asked abruptly.

"Of course," she said, curious about the question
and the somber look on his face. "I enjoy my work,
Ramon."

"I know that. But, if you had other duties to occupy you...?"

"I don't understand."

He sighed deeply. "No, I don't suppose you do.
Let it drop. It's too soon, anyway." He smiled at her.
"Sleep well."

"You, too," she replied. "You never seem to get
enough rest," she added without meaning to.

Her concern was like a warm hand on cold skin.
He smiled gently. "It never mattered," he said.
"Work was my salvation, all the long, lonely years."

"You had a hard life when you first came to this
country, didn't you?"

He nodded. "Very difficult. You'd know about
hardships and poverty, too, wouldn't you?"

"Yes. My parents were very poor. There was never
enough money."

"For some people, there never is," he said bitterly.
"Isadora had ten times as much as most women of
her class, and nothing she had ever really pleased her.

She found poor people annoying." He stared at her warmly. "I remember standing beside you in the soup kitchen, watching your face as you dished up food. All those cold, hungry, frightened people, Noreen. And so few people who give a damn."

"I know." She searched his tired face silently. "I know a lot more than that about you," she added slowly. "You've taken several cases that you never got paid for, because the people didn't have money for surgery, or insurance."

"What skill I have comes from God," he said. "A gift. One learns eventually that all gifts come at a price, part of which is sharing with the less fortunate." He searched her eyes. "I thank God even more for that skill now. You might have died."

"It wasn't my time, apparently."

"You'll never know how I felt when I saw your face without the oxygen mask, in the recovery room. All the cruelty came back to haunt me." He leaned heavily against the door facing. "We hurt you terribly at Isadora's funeral. I'll never forget the things I said to you. One day, I hope you can truly forgive me for saying them. I was eaten up with my own guilt, you see. She said she'd get even if I didn't take her. She wasn't that bad when I left."

She took a slow breath. "No, she wasn't. But she sat out in the freezing rain in a negligee for several hours. Deliberately. That was why she became so ill. The maid had to leave and I was already feeling sick. I should have phoned someone right then."

His breath caught. "Good God, why didn't you tell me?"

"You wouldn't have listened," she said simply. "She must not have known how dangerous a thing a lung infection can be. The power went off and I stumbled around trying to find the staircase, desperate to get help for her. The last thing I remember is trying to catch my balance…''

His eyes closed. ''Coals of fire,'' he whispered harshly. ''Dear God, Noreen!'' He pushed away from the door and left her, so sick inside that he couldn't even face her.

''I'm sorry,'' she said, but there was no one to hear. All the same, she thought as she laid back on the pillows, perhaps it was just as well that he finally knew the truth.

Nine

The next afternoon, Miss Plimm helped Noreen into the shower. It was difficult to take a bath at all, and tub baths weren't yet allowed. She had several incisions; one in her groin where the heart catheter had been inserted, two where the drainage tubes had been in her chest, and one in the center of her chest where the incision had been made for the actual heart surgery.

She had to bathe the incisions gently with a bacterial soap. They couldn't yet be submerged, although she'd noticed that Ramon had a huge whirlpool bath with brass fittings in the master bathroom, like something out of a Roman fantasy. Noreen had eyed it covetously on one of her walks around the large apartment with Miss Plimm and longed to soak in it. But she was at least able to take frequent showers now that she was a little steadier on her feet, and while she was in the shower, Miss Plimm helped her wash her wealth of hair.

She was back in bed, in one of her pretty embroidered white gowns, when Ramon came home early. Miss Plimm was holding the hair dryer for her, and it was taking a long time to dry the thick golden length of her hair.

"I'll do that," Ramon told Miss Plimm as he took the hair dryer from her. "You might tell cook to do something Latin for supper. I'm in the mood for fajitas or tamales. How about the two of you?"

"Sounds great to me," Miss Plimm said with a smile, and Noreen nodded her assent. "I'll see what she can rustle up. And I need to run to the store, if I have time before we eat. We're low on bacterial soap."

He reached into his wallet and handed her a bill. "Get a hair band," he added. "Or a ribbon. Something to tie up her hair with."

Miss Plimm chuckled. "I'll do that." She went out, closing the door behind her.

Noreen searched his drawn face. "Are you all right?" she asked, because she'd worried most of the day about his reaction to what she'd told him of Isadora's last hours.

"I'm fine," he said. "I wish I'd known sooner. And not only about Isadora's final act of revenge," he added, searching her eyes. "No wonder you were so bitter."

"Yes, I was," she agreed. "But as you said before, we can't live in the past. Isadora is dead. Nothing will bring her back."

"I know that. We were mismatched from the beginning, but a man is often blinded by desire." He searched Noreen's eyes. "You blended into the woodwork."

"Deliberately," she mused. "I didn't like the way Isadora got even when I made myself noticed, especially around men." She laughed coolly. "Not that anyone noticed me. And you hated me."

He didn't smile. "No." His dark eyes narrowed. "You never realized the truth. Isadora did. She accused me of being obsessed with you, did you know?"

She caught her breath. "I beg your pardon?"

He laughed. "You don't understand? I taunted you to keep you at bay. What I felt was violent. It still is."

"You still dislike me?" she asked, trying to comprehend what he was telling her.

"Good God," he breathed heavily, and just shook his head. He sat down close beside Noreen on the bed and turned on the hair dryer. One lean hand feathered her hair while the other held the dryer to blow warm air through it. He was very close. His jacket was off, the top buttons of his spotless white shirt undone, his tie off. He smelled of cologne and soap, and the nearness of that lean face, with its smooth brown surface so close, was a temptation to her lips. He had the blackest hair and eyes she'd ever seen, and the thickest eyelashes...

He sensed her scrutiny and turned his head, just the slightest bit. His black eyes searched her gray ones at such close range that shivers of pure electricity ran through her body. Her lips parted under the rapid force of her breath.

The hair dryer blew on, forgotten, until he realized he still held it. He cut it off and laid it aside, his own breath unsteady. Slowly his lean hands gathered in the length of her thick hair and savored it. He lifted it to his mouth, his eyes closed, in a silence that was all but tangible.

"I used to dream of your hair," he whispered into the stillness. "I was glad that you wore it on top of your head, because the temptation to touch it was so violent in me." His lips touched it again, almost reverently. "I thought how it would feel to hold that exquisite weight in my hands, against my lips..."

Her gasp brought his head up. He released her hair with obvious reluctance and searched her eyes slowly. "You didn't know that I was eaten up with desire for you, did you?" he asked gently.

"No," she faltered, surprised. "I...I had no idea!"

He drew in a long breath before he picked up the hair dryer and stared at it. "I could never have told you, of course," he said after a minute. "But that was why I became so sarcastic and unkind after my marriage. Making you uncomfortable kept you from getting too close." His eyes narrowed as they met her shocked ones. "In one way or another, Noreen, I seem to have spent the past six years making a torment of your life."

She stared at him with open curiosity, almost with fascination. "Are you letting me stay here as a sort of penance?" she asked.

His shoulders rose and fell. "Perhaps it began that way, but it isn't so simple a motive anymore." His eyes moved over her slender body and back up to her drawn face. "I've lived in shadows for so long, I'd forgotten how it felt to lift my face to the sun. Suddenly I enjoy coming home."

"To another patient." She laughed nervously.

"You aren't a patient. You're a treasure. I keep you under lock and key and hate sharing you with other people."

She looked up. He wasn't teasing this time. His eyes were dark and very possessive. He made her nervous, because she still didn't quite trust him.

He saw that mistrust and smiled. "All right. I'll act with more decorum, if that's what you prefer. But when you're back on your feet again and completely healed, look out," he threatened softly. "I won't give you up easily."

She frowned slightly, curious, but he'd already moved away.

"Feel like seeing your aunt and uncle?" he asked.

She grimaced. "I suppose so."

"You'll find them vastly changed," he promised. His gaze slid over her face in its setting of long, dark blond hair. "What a picture you make, like that," he murmured huskily. "I have to keep reminding myself of how fragile you still are."

"Why?" she asked without thinking.

"Because I'd like to bend you back over the pillows and kiss your body until you moaned."

She flushed. "Ramon!"

He held up a hand. "We both know that you aren't in any condition for such treatment now, so don't panic. I'm only giving you fair warning of what's coming."

"A threat?"

"Oh, no. A sweet promise," he said softly. "You might start thinking about what sort of ring you'd like."

She frowned. Perhaps she had a fever. She felt her forehead, but it was cool.

"I don't wear rings," she faltered.

He picked up her left hand and looked at the long fingers with their short nails. "Do you like white gold?" he murmured. "With rubies, perhaps, to match all that hidden fire in you."

"Why should you want to give me a ring?" she asked, still drowning in confusion.

"I like having you in my life," he said simply. "You don't have anyone, really, except Donaldson." His face tautened even as he spoke the name, and he slid his hands into his pockets impatiently. "And I don't think you love him," he added bluntly.

"I like him…very much," she protested.

"I like him, too. But he isn't the man for you. He doesn't leave you shaken and flushed when he comes out of your room."

"Why should he?" she asked bluntly.

"A prospective lover should make an impression," he replied. "He should make you tremble with delicious, forbidden thoughts and longings. He should leave you flushed with the force of your need for him. It should give you pleasure just to look at him. You show none of these signs when Donaldson visits." His eyes narrowed on her flushed face, and he noted the slight tremor of her hands when they touched the sheet covering her. "However, you show every one of them with me."

She clenched her teeth and glared at him. "I'm cold," she said doggedly, "and I think I have a fever!"

"A fever for me," he agreed, and he wasn't teasing. His face was solemn. "I feel the same fever for you, along with respect and admiration and tenderness and desire."

"I won't sleep with you," she said shortly.

"It would hardly be possible, in your condition," he agreed.

"I mean, ever!"

"Ah, now that is a long time and I am very persistent."

"I'll leave today!"

"No, you won't." He smiled at her fury. "You need rest. When Miss Plimm comes back, we'll have lunch and then your aunt and uncle can visit you just briefly. Later, when night comes, I'll read Baroja to you."

She wanted to run, but there was no place to go.

He saw the fear and understood it, perhaps better than she did. He leaned down, his eyes filling the world. "I will never hurt you again," he said poignantly. "Not physically or emotionally, nor will I ever lie to you."

"What do you want from me?" she asked in a husky whisper, because it was hard to speak with him so close that she could smell his cologne, the soap he used.

"Don't you know, Noreen?" he whispered. He bent closer and kissed her, but not with desire or lust. It was the most tender caress she could have imagined. And when he left her, she thought that perhaps she really had imagined it all.

Her aunt and uncle came just after Miss Plimm had carried away the empty soup bowl. They were pleasant, but awkward and a little nervous.

"We wanted to come sooner," her uncle said, "but Ramon told us to wait a bit, until you were stronger."

He leaned forward in his chair. "Do you have everything you need?"

"Oh, yes," she agreed. "Ramon's taken very good care of me. I'm his patient," she added quickly, so they wouldn't think she was trying to take their daughter's place in his life.

Mary Kensington looked older and much less self-assured. "Isadora is dead," she said in a quiet voice. "We made a saint of her because it hurt so badly when she died, but she was just a woman, Noreen, not a saint. We know how it was between her and Ramon, so don't think you're treading on anyone's sacred memories by being here in his apartment." She smiled sadly. "I'm only sorry that we didn't know how dangerous your own situation was. It still hurts to remember how we treated you after Isadora's death. It always will. I hope you can forgive us."

"We'd like to do something for you," her uncle added. "Anything we can." He looked very uncomfortable. "It isn't easy for us to admit what idiots we've been."

They both looked so miserable that she couldn't hold out against them. She was far too softhearted. "Maybe I should have tried harder to make you listen," Noreen said after a minute, her tone warmer. "I'm not completely innocent. She did die, because of me."

"She died because God decided it was her time to die," Mary said quietly. "We've changed in the past two years. Perhaps you don't know, but it wasn't to stem gossip that we invited you over just before your uncle's birthday. We were trying to mend fences."

Her uncle flushed and couldn't look at her, remembering the foul remark he'd made to Ramon about the present Noreen had bought him. "We weren't trying very hard," he admitted with a self-conscious smile. "But we are now. We'd like to have you around whenever you want to come and visit. It's pretty lonely for us these days."

"It is for me, too," Noreen admitted. She looked at them quietly, realizing how tired and worn they both were. She could hardly blame them for loving their daughter to distraction. "I'd like to visit you, when I'm able."

"We could go down to the Caribbean," Mary suggested with quiet pleasure. "It would do you good to be lazy in the sun and relax. Your job must be a hard one."

"It is," Noreen said. "But it's one that I love."

"Still," her uncle added, "you won't be able to work for a couple of months, will you? Nothing wrong with a vacation in the meantime."

She was hesitant, not because she wasn't grateful, but because she'd just realized that sooner or later she was going to have to leave Ramon.

"Think about it," Mary encouraged. "You don't have to decide right now."

"I will. Thank you."

They were still a little awkward when they left, but the atmosphere was the best it had ever been. In time, Noreen thought, they might become close.

Ramon came back when they left to see how the visit had affected his patient. He had a stethoscope in his hand and Miss Plimm was with him.

"I just want to check you," he reassured her, motioning Miss Plimm to do the necessary uncovering.

It surprised Noreen that he had Miss Plimm stay while he examined her, but perhaps he was regretting

the wild statements he'd made earlier and didn't want
Noreen to get any ideas about his intentions. Here, he
had a witness who could swear that he hadn't touched
Noreen in any unprofessional way.

He lifted his head and nodded. "That valve sounds
very good. Of course, we'll need to monitor you
closely for the first few weeks."

"My aunt and uncle want to take me on a holiday
down to the Caribbean," she ventured.

His eyes darkened. "Not right away," he said.
"I'll want you close to the hospital. Not because I
expect anything to go wrong," he added harshly
when he saw her expression, "simply because it isn't
wise to leave the country only a few days after major
surgery!"

"Oh. I see."

"You could have fooled me," he said curtly. "I'll
check on you again later. No trips. Not until you're
released, and that won't be until three months after
the date of the surgery. Maybe."

He turned on his heel and walked out. Noreen
didn't know why he was so angry. Surely he didn't
mind that her aunt and uncle were trying to build a
relationship with her.

He left and didn't come back until almost bedtime.
He'd been working, she could tell by the drawn look
about him.

"Emergency surgery," he explained, all but falling
into the chair by the bed. "And not in time. He didn't
make it. I had to tell his pregnant wife." He hit the
arm of the chair with the flat of his hand. "Damn it,
why don't people think? He'd known for years that
he had a bad heart, but he refused to go to the doctor,

even when he started having shortness of breath and chest pain. He collapsed at the office and when they brought him in, the major part of his heart was already dead. Dead! You can't replace dead heart tissue and it doesn't regenerate. I couldn't do a thing for him. Damn the luck!''

He was furious, but underneath it was a black grief that he hadn't been able to save the man.

Noreen simply held out her arms.

At first he couldn't believe his own eyes. Then he drew in a ragged breath and went to her, careful not to put any pressure on her chest as he buried his face in her long, soft hair and gripped the pillows beside her head. She felt a wetness on his cheek where she stroked it and smiled sadly. It was one of the many things she loved about Ramon, that he didn't stoically hide every emotion and pretend he felt nothing. He wasn't less a man for being able to feel compassion.

''It's all right,'' she whispered, smoothing his thick black hair. ''I know you did the very best you could do. But God decides in the end who lives and who dies. Not even the best surgeon can stand against God. It's not your fault, Ramon. It's not your fault.''

Her voice was comforting. He loved the softness of it. He drew in a steadying breath and seemed to relax in her arms. ''You were raised Catholic, weren't you?'' he asked suddenly, his voice deep and quiet.

Her hand stilled in his hair. ''Yes. But later on, I went with my aunt and uncle to the Presbyterian church. I still go, when I'm not working.''

He lifted his head and searched her eyes. His were still damp, but he didn't seem to mind her seeing them. He brushed the disheveled hair away from her cheek. ''I don't go to mass as often as I should, or to confession. But I feel my faith deeply. At times like these, it sustains me."

Her fingertips traced his firm chin. He was so good to look at. "I know it hurts to lose a patient. You have to try to think about how many lives you've saved," she said softly, "instead of dwelling on the ones that don't live." She smiled gently. "It hurts me to lose a patient, too, even though I'm a nurse. Despite all they tell us about keeping an emotional distance, it's impossible not to get attached to some people."

He drew in a long breath and toyed with her hair. "That's true." He smiled.

She loved touching him. Her eyes betrayed the tenderness she couldn't hide. He saw it, and his chest rose and fell unsteadily.

"You love children, don't you?" he asked. "I remember seeing you on the pediatric cancer ward last Christmas, playing with the toddlers and then crying in the hall afterward."

She remembered that Ramon had spotted her there, and despite the enmity between them, he'd stopped long enough to talk to her. In fact, he'd spent several minutes with her there in the corridor, talking softly about the new treatments, the experimental drugs. He'd talked until the tears stopped, and he'd been kind. It hadn't occurred to her at the time how odd it was to have her worst enemy offer kindness.

"They were so young," she said. "So terribly young to have known that kind of pain and hopelessness."

"One day research will catch up with cancer," he promised her.

"Oh, I hope so." She searched his eyes. "Feel better?" she asked softly.

He smiled and nodded. "Much."

"Have you eaten?"

He shook his head. "I wasn't hungry. But I think I could eat now. Have you had anything?"

"I had some of the cook's potato and broccoli soup. It was delicious."

"I think I'll go and have a bowl of it. Can I bring you anything?"

"No, thank you. Have you seen Mosquito?" she asked suddenly, having missed the kitten.

"She's in the kitchen having a snack," he said. He took her hand in his and brought it to his lips. "Have you noticed how we nurture each other?" he asked softly.

She flushed. "I would have done the same thing for…"

"For anyone?" he asked. "Yes, I know. But perhaps not in the same way." He bent and touched his cool lips gently to her mouth. "Do you want to hear Baroja, when I've eaten?"

She smiled. "Yes."

"I'll be back in a few minutes."

He got up from the bed and gazed down at her hungrily. He'd never had such tender comfort in his life as she gave him. He'd lost a patient early in his marriage to Isadora, and his depression had only irritated her. She was getting ready for a dinner party and chided him for being so involved with his patients. She'd never understood, as Noreen did, his pain at being incapable of holding back the Grim Reaper.

"Are you all right now?" she asked.

He smiled at her. "Yes. I'm all right. I'll be back when I've eaten."

And he was. He read her the first chapter of *Paradox, Rey* by Baroja, pausing as he went along to let her translate. She understood most of it, and he helped her when she had problems with some unfamiliar verbs.

"I especially like the part, later on, with the feminist who swears that Shakespeare was a woman." She chuckled.

He laughed along with her. "Yes. It's a marvelous work, isn't it? He was brilliant, despite his idiosyncrasies."

"You read Spanish so beautifully," she remarked. "I could listen to you all night. But you need your rest."

He closed the book. "So do you. Is it still sore?"

She grimaced. "Yes, but it's where the stitches were that bother me most. They're starting to itch, and they're uncomfortable."

"I used staples," he reminded her, "not stitches."

"Whatever it is itches."

He chuckled. "That means it's healing," he reassured her. "Need something to help you sleep?"

"A couple of those pain tablets would be nice," she admitted. "I won't get addicted or anything?"

"As if I'd be negligent enough to let you," he chided. He shook out the tablets from the prescription bottle into her hand and helped her with the glass of juice to swallow them.

"Sorry," she murmured. "I know better."

"Of course you do." He put the glass away. "Sleep well."

"When can I get outside again?" she asked.

"Perhaps next week, on a sunny day. We'll talk about it later."

"I want to see the world outside."

"I'll do my best to get you out there," he promised. "But I can't let you catch cold. You'll have to dress warmly. Do you have a coat at your apartment?"

She grimaced. "A jacket."

He didn't say anything. He only murmured, and shortly thereafter he left.

A week later, on a sunny day, he helped her into a new full-length velvet coat the color of sapphires. She started to protest, but he told her that it was one he'd found on sale and it was only a trifle. She could even pay him back if she was determined to be independent. Thankfully she couldn't get to the exclusive boutique where he'd purchased it to see the price tag.

She gave in gracefully and clung to his arm as he escorted her into the elevator and then out the front door. The apartment manager and the clerk watched their slow progress with wide grins. Everyone who knew Ramon had learned about the care he was taking of his cousin-in-law. It was nice to see her up and around after so frightening a surgery. Ramon was well liked, and so was Miss Plimm, who could be encouraged to talk about her nice young patient.

Ramon helped her slowly through the revolving door and onto the street where she was almost knocked down by an irritated-looking businessman who glared at her.

"She's just had open-heart surgery," Ramon told the man with a threat in his black eyes. "You might have enough consideration for other pedestrians to slow down!''

The man took a good look at Noreen and flushed a little as he saw the effort it was taking her just to walk.

''Sorry,'' he murmured and with a quick glance at Ramon he darted inside.

''The eternal businessman,'' Ramon muttered. ''How little money compares to good health. I expect his blood pressure runs high and he fills his system with fried foods and takeout.''

''Boy, are you in a foul mood,'' she chided breathlessly, clinging to him in the soft coat and fuzzy hat he'd bought her to go with it.

He held her more securely, his dark eyes still flashing with temper as he looked down at her. ''He might have hurt you,'' he said angrily.

She liked his protective attitude, because she was weak and fragile and vulnerable. Quick tears rose in her eyes.

''Stop that,'' he said softly, wiping them away with a gloved hand. ''A miss is as good as a mile.''

''That wasn't why,'' she explained, searching his eyes. ''I was thinking how sweet it was to have you concerned for me, that's all. It frightened me a little.''

His jaw went taut. ''I should have knocked him down,'' he gritted.

She drew two long breaths. ''I'm all right, as long as I've got you to hold onto.'' She clung to his arm, smiling, radiant. ''Oh, Ramon, it's so nice to be outside!''

The face she turned up to his was so beautiful that it hit him in the stomach like a fist. He actually caught his breath at its utter loveliness.

"Is something wrong?" she asked.

He shook his head. "Nothing at all," he assured her. "I was thinking how lovely you look."

She flushed. "The coat and hat are very nice."

"The woman inside them is beautiful," he replied. "And not only outwardly. I was also thinking," he added, "how sweet it would be if we had a little girl with your big gray eyes and that soft, sweet smile."

Ten

She felt the ground go out from under her, and his supporting arm was there, gently holding her up.

"It's too soon for this," he said at once, worried. "I shouldn't have let you walk so far."

"I'm all right," she replied. She leaned against him. "It wasn't the walking. I thought I heard you say…" She laughed self-consciously. "Never mind. I expect I'm a little disoriented."

"I said that I'd like to have a daughter with you," he repeated it, bringing her startled gaze up to his. "I quite realize that it's much too soon to be speaking of such things. But we've spoken of rings, and babies seemed the natural end to the sequence."

"Rings…you meant a…a wedding ring?" she exclaimed.

He scowled. "Of what were you thinking?"

"A Christmas present," she faltered. "Perhaps a birthstone ring."

He sighed roughly. "I suppose I can't expect you to trust me so completely all at once, much less expect talk of marriage," he asked with scarcely concealed impatience.

She shook her head. She was certain that she must be losing her mind. Her wide gray eyes were fixed, unblinking, on his lean, handsome face.

His gaze went from her face down her slender body in the long coat. "A surgeon's life is a hectic one," he said, holding her gently just in front of him while pedestrians went around them. "But I have some time to myself, as you see, and I make more than enough to support you and a family."

Her cheeks felt hot. "You only feel guilty and sorry for me..."

He smiled gently. "Two emotions that have no power to induce a proposal of marriage from me, Noreen," he said. "We fit together so well, haven't you noticed? You're happy with me, aren't you?"

She was worried. Her hands pressed into the cashmere of his long coat. "Yes." There was no denying that. "But it's too soon. I want to be back on my feet and completely well before we..." She looked up. "Can I have a baby?"

His cheeks actually flushed.

She glowered at him. "Not right now," she muttered. "I mean, will I be able to, with an artificial valve?"

"Of course," he said. He laughed unsteadily. "My God, what a knock you gave me." He caught his breath. "Forgive me. I immediately thought of ways and means around your condition. Which is an utter impossibility at the moment, anyway."

Now she blushed and looked away, understanding him all too well.

"You could answer me, though," he prompted.

She moved closer to him. "I love babies."

"I know. So do I."

"And I suppose it would be best if they came in wedlock instead of outside it. But my aunt and uncle…"

"Would be delighted," he assured her. "They love children, too. It was their greatest hope to one day have grandchildren." He drew in a short breath. "Something they would never have known with Isadora. She disliked children."

Her eyes lifted to his hard face. It was hard to see Ramon as a serious suitor. She couldn't help but think that he was somewhat in the position of guardian and he liked taking care of someone. That was nice, and she enjoyed it, but it wasn't love. She couldn't marry without it, especially not in his faith, which didn't really consider divorce a legitimate means of resolving differences, however great.

He touched her face gently, sensing her indecision. "Give it time. All I ask is that you think about it."

"I will," she promised.

"And now," he murmured with a wry glance around them, "I think it might be a good idea if we walk a little and stop blocking traffic."

She laughed breathlessly, clinging to his arm. "Okay."

He walked her slowly to the corner and let her rest before they went along. She was winded and flushed, but that was natural. Instinctively his hand dropped to her wrist, counting her pulse. It was strong, and the rhythm was as regular as could be expected at this point of her recovery. He smiled. "The exercise will get easier," he promised.

It did. He walked with her every day, except when he had emergencies. Days turned to weeks, and weeks to months. She recovered her strength, her spirit and her chest stopped hurting. He still read to her at night, despite her improved condition, his voice soft and tender in the stillness of the apartment. He shared his worries with her. He cherished her. But he kept his distance, physically, and Noreen began to wonder if he was having second thoughts about his impulsive statement on the first day they'd walked, about wanting to marry her.

He'd had one bad marriage already. He wouldn't want to risk a second one. And Noreen was more or less thrust upon him as a patient. She couldn't shake the feeling, despite his protests, that he was trying to make amends for his bitter treatment of her. If that were the case, then his coolness might well be doubts seeping in about their future together.

All the same, he watched her like a hawk, making sure that she kept appointments with the cardiologist, had her blood-clotting time checked weekly, took her medicine. His partner, who saw Noreen for her office visit, and her cardiologist both agreed that she was well enough not only to drive, but to go back to work. But Ramon went through the ceiling the minute she mentioned that to him, after her preliminary check-ups.

Miss Plimm had been dismissed, reluctantly, because Noreen was no longer in need of a nurse. And it was a good thing, because his angry voice carried all over the apartment. Whatever reserve he'd been showing until now went into total eclipse. He was furious, Latin temper, cursing in two languages and demanding to know what idiocy she was contemplating.

She tried to reason with him. "It isn't that I'm not grateful for all you've done for me, but you're not responsible for my upkeep. I want to earn my own living. I have an apartment that they've been holding for me since the surgery..."

"You don't need to be living by yourself," he argued. "It's too soon."

"I've been here for three months!" she exclaimed. "Everyone says I'm more than able to go back to work. My pro-time checks out like clockwork, I'm walking every day, I eat like a horse...why are you being so difficult?"

He threw up his hands, muttering something in Spanish about trying to argue with walls.

"I am not a wall," she snapped back, hands on her hips.

Despite his anger, his eyes twinkled at her spirit. She'd been like a shadow of herself when she was so ill, and he'd worried himself sick about leaving her there even with Miss Plimm. But now, she had good color, her heart was working almost as good as new—possibly better—and she was certainly able to work, at least part-time. He wished he had a better excuse to keep her here. He didn't know how he was going to bear living in the apartment alone.

"You can't take Mosquito with you," he said finally, searching for an argument that would stop her from leaving. He faced her with his hands deep in his pockets. "She'll grieve."

"Nonsense," she said without any real conviction. She was going to grieve, too, for the cat but mostly for Ramon. But she had to be sure that what he felt for her wasn't pity. She couldn't ever know at this close range. She wanted them both to step back and be objective. The time they'd spent together might have blinded Ramon to his true feelings.

His lean face had an expression that was harder than she'd seen in years. "You aren't going to be happy alone," he said angrily.

She didn't deny it. What would have been the point? She simply looked at him, with eyes that expected pain. "You've learned a lot of things about the past that you didn't know before," she began hesitantly. "It was inevitable that you might feel some guilt. And as you said yourself, you've never really had anyone to take care of."

His chin lifted. "In other words, you think that proximity has blinded me to my own feelings."

She nodded.

He drew in a long, slow breath. "I see."

"I'm more grateful than I can say that you've taken such wonderful care of me," she told him. "But we both know that you'd have been just as kind to a total stranger. It's the way you are."

"You flatter me. And you denigrate your own worth," he added. "Perhaps I've caused you to expect so little from life. I've made you bitter."

His accent was more noticeable, as if he found it difficult to say these things. He looked so utterly defeated that he made her feel guilty.

"I'm not bitter anymore," she said quietly. "Aunt

Mary and Uncle Hal have been wonderful to me. I'll enjoy visiting them now.''

"Don't let them take you out of the country,'' he said firmly. "It's too soon.''

"Your partner said it would be fine!'' she said, exasperated.

"Why are you listening to him?'' he demanded. "What does he know about your condition? I operated on you!''

His eyes were flashing like black lightning. He fascinated her in this mood.

"You'll be a case when your children are old enough to leave home,'' she observed dryly.

"How can I have children? You're leaving me!''

Her heart jumped, but she stood firm. "Just give it time,'' she said soothingly. "You'll be fine.''

"Fine!'' he scoffed. He ran a hand through his thick black hair. "Who'll be here when I need to talk? Who'll comfort me when I lose patients?''

It was hard to stand on her resolve, but she had to. She touched his arm gently. "I'm as close as the telephone,'' she promised. "You can call whenever you like. You're my friend now,'' she added without quite meeting his gaze. "Friends talk to each other.''

He didn't speak for a minute. His fingers touched her face lightly and he seemed not to breathe as he bent to brush his mouth tenderly over her own.

"You want to be my friend? Then shoot me,'' he whispered against her lips. "It would be an act of kindness.''

"Don't be absurd. I could never hurt you.''

"What do you call walking out of my life?'' he demanded.

"Self-preservation,'' she murmured.

His arms slid around her and he drew her as close as he dared, mindful of the surgery and the soreness that remained despite the healing of her breastbone.

His cheek pressed against hers and he held her, bending over her in the silence of the apartment. She gave in to him, hungry for the contact even as she knew she was making the right decision by leaving the apartment.

Inevitably his mouth slid down to possess hers in a light, soft kiss that grew deeper and more insistent by the second. She heard his deep, harsh groan instants before his tongue thrust deep into her mouth and he lifted her completely off the floor in his arms.

She couldn't resist him. Her arms went around his neck and she gave back the kiss with the same intensity that his passion demanded.

When she felt the tremor work its way through him, she withdrew just a breath and felt his mouth cling before it was able to lift.

He was breathing heavily. The eyes that looked into hers from mere inches away were black and hungry.

"If I were less scrupulous," he said huskily, "I would carry you to bed and love you until you begged to stay with me. But you are still *una virgen,* yes?"

"Yes," she whispered brokenly.

The shudder grew worse. He rested his forehead against hers, holding her gently to his chest, completely off the floor. "And this sweet condition is because of me, also, yes?" he whispered.

She bit her lip. "You are conceited."

"I'm starving," he breathed into her mouth as he kissed it yet again. "Starving to be loved, to be wanted, to be needed, to be comforted…you show me heaven and then consign me to hell, for the sake of a job!''

''Oh, no, not for that,'' she said quickly, touching his mouth, his cheek, his long, arrogant nose. ''Not for a job. I love you!''

''Querida!'' he groaned, and kissed her with aching hunger, drowning in the soft, sweet words that he'd never dared hope to hear her say to him after all the pain he'd given her.

She dragged her mouth from under his and pressed it into his hot throat, clinging to him, unmindful of any discomfort where the incision was. ''You have to let me go,'' she whispered miserably.

''Why?''

She loved the deep, tender voice so close at her ear. ''So that you'll know how you feel.''

There was a slight pause, a hesitation. He lifted his head and looked into her soft, sad eyes for a long time. ''How *I* feel?'' he asked.

She nodded.

His breath sighed out slowly. ''How can you not know?'' he asked heavily, searching her face. ''Isadora knew. She taunted me with it. I told you this.''

''You told me that she accused you of being obsessed with me,'' she agreed. ''Physically.''

He laughed softly. ''Physically?'' His eyes slid over her face and down to her body in his arms and back up again. ''There is a song, Noreen,'' he said tenderly. ''It was nominated for an Academy Award. I can't sing, *enamorada,* but the words say that when a man loves a woman, really loves her, he can see his unborn children in her eyes.''

''Yes,'' she whispered, shaken not only by the poignant words, but by the way he said them.

"To my shame, I saw my sons in your eyes the day I found you in the kitchen at your aunt's house," he whispered, watching her face color. "And I was married. What a living hell it was, to know such a sin and be unable to repent it." His eyes closed. "I paid for it and made you pay for it. And we are both still paying for it."

She didn't think she could breathe ever again. She stared at him, her eyes like saucers.

His eyes opened, looking straight into hers. Nothing was hidden, nothing was concealed. His heart was in them.

"You wanted to marry me because you loved me?" she asked in a husky voice.

"Yes," he said simply. His eyes adored her face. "I will love you forever. With my heart, my soul, my very life."

She felt the first tear before it cascaded down her pale cheek. It was followed by another, and another, silent and poignant.

"No," he whispered, kissing them away. "No. Hush, now. Don't cry. If you want to leave so badly, I won't stop you. But we must see each other, at least...Noreen!"

Her arms were around his neck so tightly that he was afraid she was going to hurt herself. She clung, crying in agonized shudders, completely at the mercy of her emotions.

"*Enamorada,*" he breathed piteously, and his lips pressed soft, tender kisses on her wet face. "Ah, don't cry. Don't. I can't bear to hear you cry like this."

"I thought you hated me," she sobbed.

"Yes. I had to let you think so. It would have been

dishonorable to admit such feelings. I was married. In my faith, marriage is for life.''

"I know." She rubbed her wet cheek against his. "That's why I was going to leave. I didn't want you to be stuck with me after you came to your senses. I thought you only pitied me.''

He held her close and his chest rose in a great sigh. "I loved you," he said. "I meant every word I said. I want to spend the rest of my life with you. I want children with you.''

"I want them with you, too," she confessed. "I was trying to be noble.''

"Nobility is best left to saints," he said pointedly. He lifted his head and looked into her wet eyes. "I think we should be married as soon as possible," he said.

"Do you?"

He nodded. "You have this tendency to run away," he said, smiling. "Perhaps if you marry me, you will be content to stay at home.''

Her fingers toyed with the thick hair at his nape. "I could do relief work," she murmured.

He studied her closely. "Until the babies come?''

She smiled shyly. "Until then. And after they start school. I do like my job.''

"You do it very well.''

"You didn't always think so," she reminded him.

He made a face at her. "Drag up my ghosts to haunt me," he accused.

She kissed his firm mouth gently. "Sorry.''

"Oh, no, I'm not so easily placated as that," he murmured, bending to her lips. "I have to be appeased.''

"Like this?" she whispered, and kissed him with slow, insistent pleasure.

He returned the kiss with equal intensity until they were both shaken.

He lifted his head. "My heart, this kissing is a dangerous thing." He searched her eyes. "We will be married in church," he said. "And you will wear a white gown, and a veil. And afterward, we will have a wedding night."

She colored delicately. "Most people think we already have, or so I've heard from Brad."

He lifted an eyebrow. "Has he been to visit again?"

She grinned. "Just for a few minutes. And before you jump to conclusions, he's very much in love with someone at the hospital. Not me," she added before he could speak. "We're friends. That's all we've ever been."

"You can be friends from a safe distance from now on," he said firmly.

"Why, you're jealous," she accused.

"Very." He kissed her. "And also very tired." He chuckled, placing her back on her feet with a grimace. "Even this small weight grows heavy with the passage of time. But I promise to carry you over the threshhold after we are married."

"I'll hold you to that," she said, smiling with her whole heart.

He touched her face gently, savoring the love in her eyes. "I have dreamed of holding you in the darkness, in my arms. The reality of it is more than I dared hope for." He traced her lips. "And such a gift you bring to the marriage bed. I hope to be worthy of it."

She hid her face against his chest, embarrassed despite her years as a nurse.

He smoothed her back under his lean hands. "You aren't afraid?"

"No," she whispered, closing her eyes. "I adore you."

"And I, you." He kissed her hair.

Their marriage was announced and planned, and all the things that had worried Noreen vanished in the euphoria of loving and being loved. Everything fell into place. The greatest surprise was the pleasure the news gave to Noreen's aunt and uncle. Aunt Mary immediately took over the preparations and planning, and by the end of the week, she had it all arranged, right down to the invitations and the cake and the reception. Noreen was in awe of her ability to organize.

Of course, there was no question of Noreen going back to work now. Her whole life seemed to suddenly center around fittings for her wedding gown and sending out invitations. She and her aunt grew close during this time, because Ramon had insisted that she move into her aunt and uncle's home now that they were engaged. He wanted, he told her, no improprieties at all to shadow their married lives, and no gossip. This amused everyone who knew him, but no one more than Noreen herself.

He carried that decision to extremes, refusing to touch her at all until the vows were spoken. He was far more rigid in his views than she'd imagined, but his tenderness with her was an everlasting source of pleasure and delight.

She blossomed in their new relationship, and so did

he. The nurses teased him when he made rounds, although he noticed that Brad Donaldson was a little hesitant about approaching him once he knew Ramon and Noreen were engaged. That amused him. All the same, it was just as well that the man had stopped coming to visit Noreen. Ramon was a tolerant man, but not when it came to the woman he loved. Her friends from now on, he assured himself, were going to be female, not male.

Ramon took Noreen out to dinner several times before the wedding, always meticulously correct in his behavior. But in his eyes smoldered such fires that she became a little wary of him.

The night before their wedding, he put an arm across her as she started to open the car door in her aunt's driveway.

"You become more nervous of me by the day," he said softly. He eased his long fingers in between hers. "Tell me why."

She leaned against him and his arm enfolded her to his chest. "I don't know much about men," she confessed. "Is it going to be all right? I mean, you look at me as if you could eat me alive, and I'm not sure I'll be enough for you."

He chuckled softly. "You'll be enough," he assured her. "But I confess I was having fears of my own, about you."

She looked up. "About me?"

"Innocence is daunting to me," he told her gently. "Your body will have to be hungry enough for mine that I won't hurt you."

She nuzzled her face against him. "It will be. That isn't what worries me at all."

"Ah, here we have it," he murmured against her

temple. "You think I have had a succession of women in my life, hmm?"

"You were in your early thirties when you married Isadora."

He traced her cheek and then tugged her chin up to make her look at him. "I was faithful to my wife. After she died, there was no one." He touched her face with loving hands. "And after you, there will never be another."

She linked her arms around his neck and laid against him with pure delight. "We'll live happily ever after," she murmured.

"A myth," he whispered. "But if two people work at a marriage, it lasts."

"Ours will last forever," she told him.

He nodded solemnly. "Yes. I think it will."

She kissed him tenderly, to find him rigidly controlled as he put her away from him. "Don't you like kissing me anymore?" she asked.

He laughed tautly. "I like it too much. Tomorrow night, you can reasonably expect kisses, and much more."

"I like the 'much more' part very much," she whispered.

He chuckled. "So do I. And now, good night!"

"Good night." She gave him one long, last look and got out of the car.

Eleven

The wedding was an event, even though it wasn't a huge social one. Ramon and Noreen spoke their vows in front of a priest. In attendance were Ramon and Noreen's colleagues and friends from the hospital, and Noreen's aunt and uncle. Afterward, there was a small, but delightful reception at the Kensington's home.

Noreen went into the bedroom that had been hers to freshen up and put on her neat suit, in which she would travel with Ramon to Charleston, South Carolina, for a brief honeymoon. She stared at her face in the mirror, seeing nothing remarkable about its familiar contours. But the eyes, the big gray eyes, were full of joy.

She gave a thought to poor Isadora, who had never really known happiness. It was a shame that her life had been ended so abruptly, so tragically. Noreen thought that she would always feel some small guilt about Isadora's loss. If only she'd been able to make the doctor understand how desperately ill her cousin was, ask him to send an ambulance. But that wasn't to be. Somehow, she had to live with the memory and get past it, so that her own life with Ramon could begin in truth.

The door opened behind her and Mary Kensington came in, dressed in a very becoming pale blue suit with a pink silk shell beneath it. She smiled at her niece.

"Can I help?" she asked.

Noreen shook her head. She turned from the mirror. "I was thinking about Isadora," she said sadly.

Mary's eyes clouded, but only for an instant. "Noreen, none of us can change the past," she said quietly. "As I grow older, I'm more convinced than ever that things happen the way they're meant to. We all failed Isadora. Your uncle and I should never have gone off and left you by yourself to look after her. Neither should Ramon. Yours is the very least of the blame, because you could have died that night trying to take care of her. None of us were aware of how desperately ill you were. I hope you know that no one blames you in the least anymore." Her face was solemn. "I wish I could tell you how bitterly your uncle and I regret the way we treated you at Isadora's funeral. I'm sure Ramon feels exactly the same."

"You didn't know," she replied.

Mary smiled sadly. "I didn't know a lot of things. I used you shamelessly over the years. You should have made me see how selfish I was, instead of accepting meekly whatever responsibility I placed on your shoulders."

Noreen smiled back. "I never minded doing whatever I could for you. You gave me a home when my parents died. You didn't have to. You could have put me in an orphanage."

"The very idea," Mary muttered. "That would never have happened. Family is family."

"I was never abused or badly treated here, nevertheless," Noreen continued.

"But you were never really happy, either. I hope you will be now, Noreen," she said sincerely. "You and Ramon."

Impulsively Noreen went forward and awkwardly kissed her aunt on her soft, powdered cheek. "Thank you."

Mary hugged her warmly. "You're the only daughter I have left now," she said a little awkwardly. "I hope you'll come and see us from time to time. Especially when the children come along," she added, with eyes that warmed with the thought.

Noreen smiled. "We hope to have several."

"Which will give us all something to look forward to," Mary replied. "And now, we'd better get you back to your new husband. He's looking just a little impatient!"

The drive to Charleston was long, but it afforded them a privacy they could never have achieved in an airplane. Ramon stopped frequently along the way to let Noreen get out and stretch her legs, so the journey wouldn't be too tiring.

Once, they stopped to have pie and coffee, and he held her hand while she ate hers, as if he couldn't bear to let go of it.

The way he looked at her was even clearer evidence of a love he was no longer denying. The warmth in his black eyes made her heart race like mad.

He felt her pulse increase and he smiled secretively. "And now," he said softly, "you belong to me in every way. It is the happiest day of my life."

"And of mine," she agreed huskily. She searched his face with possessive eyes. "I love you."

"I love you, *querida*," he said quietly. "With all I am."

She flushed a little, still shy with him despite the beautiful gold band on her left hand, above which an engagement ring of blue topaz surrounded by diamonds sparkled in the light.

Ramon, too, wore a wide gold band. It had been his own decision, but it made her happy to think that he wanted the world to know his status as much as she did.

"I hope Mosquito won't tear up too much of Aunt Mary's furniture," she murmured. "Perhaps we should have boarded her."

"We'd come home to find her hanging from the ceiling in a net," he chuckled. "She'll be very happy with your aunt and uncle. They like her, too."

She clasped his hand and looked at him with fascination. "I still can't believe it," she said absently. "It's like having every single dream of my life come true." She frowned. "You don't think I'm dreaming?"

He smiled indulgently. "Wait until we arrive at our destination," he said softly. "And I'll prove to you that you're not."

She pressed her hand into his hungrily and her eyes searched his. "I want to be as close to you as we can be," she said shyly, dropping her gaze when she saw the fierce dark flames suddenly burning in his.

His breath sounded strained. "You take my breath away," he whispered. "But, in all honesty," he added huskily, "it is what I want as well, to feel you so close…" He bit back the rest of what he was going to say and finished his pie.

They arrived at the luxury hotel in Charleston a short time later. Neither had spoken very much in the car, in a tense and hungry atmosphere that was almost tangible.

Ramon checked them in with seeming patience and then tipped the bellboy who had carried their luggage to their suite. But no sooner was the door closed and locked behind the man than Ramon had Noreen up in his arms and headed straight for the king-size bed. He didn't even stop to turn down the covers, so hungry was he for the feel and touch and taste of her.

"Is it…too soon?" he whispered at her eager lips. "Are you tired…?"

Her long legs wrapped around his as much as her skirt permitted and her mouth gave him her answer. The nervousness she'd felt at first was completely gone, replaced by a passion so long denied on both sides that it was overwhelming.

It was explosive between them, hungry and hot and so frantic that she couldn't even think.

One minute they were fully clothed, and the next they were so close that she could feel him in every cell of her body. He savored her warm, soft nudity with his mouth, his hands, his eyes.

Her hands touched him with wonder, enjoying the feel of his warm bronzed body all along her own. He watched her with eyes that grew each second more hungry.

Slowly, then, the practiced caresses became more invasive, more drugging. He smoothed her down on the bed and his mouth found her in ways that all her imagining hadn't prepared her for. She gasped, and he laughed softly at her shock, and then increased the pressure of his mouth against her taut breasts, slowly, so slowly, drawing the hard nipples into his mouth to taste them with his tongue.

She was more than ready for him when the need became too great to prolong.

He eased over her, his arms catching his weight as he made of his entire lean body one long caress, holding her gaze all the while to watch the wonder and shock and delight in them when he began to join his body to hers.

"Is it what you expected, ¿querida?" he whispered as his hips moved down to hers. "Are you frightened of me, like this?"

She felt the power and strength of him against her softness with awe and just a little fear. Her hands tightened on his shoulders. She swallowed, her lips parting as he moved gently on a nervous breath.

"Does it hurt?" he persisted, his face showing the strain of his restraint for her sake.

She bit her lower lip. "It...burns," she whispered, reddening.

"Yes. But it will ease," he whispered back, his voice deep in the room, the silence unbroken except for the sound of their unsteady breathing. His hand moved between them and he touched her gently, anticipating her shocked momentary withdrawal.

"I'm sorry." She laughed nervously.

"No, it is I who should be sorry, for rushing you," he said gently. He smiled and touched her softly, in a totally new way, so that her body clenched, but not in pain. "Yes," he said, watching her eyes. "This is what was missing, this tension that builds sweetly, that makes your body so hungry for me that even pain is no deterrent... Ah, yes. There. And there..."

She was clutching him with her fingernails, holding on for dear life, because the pleasure he was giving her now made her moan with a new hunger. She wanted him to touch her again and again, she wanted to feel his hands seeking... Oh, there! There!

"Ramon!" she sobbed. Her hands seemed at once to be pulling him and pushing him. Her long legs wrapped without inhibition around his and she moved, lifted...

Her eyes flew open as she felt him. She was shocked, speechless, despite all the lectures and all the books she'd read. Nothing in her experience described the sensations that were throbbing along her every nerve as he moved in a slow, gentle rhythm and her body began to adjust to him. There was a slight hesitation, with a flash of pain that she barely recognized as such, and then all at once, he was completely part of her.

She absorbed him, and then lay shaking with her heartbeat, looking up into his eyes as they moved as one body in a slow, steady, sweet rhythm that all at once became desperation. She clung as a piercing, throbbing pleasure took her higher than she'd ever been in her life. She sobbed, watching his face contort as he, too, found the source of the hot pleasure and gave himself to it. They stilled for that one long second of shared pleasure and stared at each other, breathless in their staggering closeness.

"Incredible," he breathed, his face hard with contained passion.

She searched his eyes, tense with her own need. "Yes."

"Can you, again?" he whispered tenderly.

"I can," she managed to say through her breathless delight. "I'm fine." She looked down and flushed as he did the same.

"It was never like this," he said, trying to explain the enormity of what he was feeling. "Never!"

He moved with exquisite tenderness and heard her breath catch. He smiled, and moved again, and bent to her mouth. The need was still there, but it transmuted into a slow, soft, incredibly intimate rhythm that both worked to keep from becoming frantic. He looked into her eyes as the ecstasy began to grip him, laughing with shock as he felt the glory of it wash over him in slow, dragging waves that prolonged what was already unbearable joy.

She laughed with him and then groaned and sobbed as she gave herself to the feverish heat and arched up into his waiting body, giving up her body and her heart in the same crisp, oblivious little movement.

It was like riding a rainbow, drowning in warm wine, breathing joy. She clung to him, shuddering, and clung still harder, because the ecstasy never seemed to end. Her muscles hurt from the tension, but it was too sweet to fight.

Eventually she was too exhausted to withstand the pressure, and she fell back away from him, trembling in the aftermath. His own pleasure long since achieved, he smiled down at her, having sustained her for as long as she was capable of receiving pleasure from him.

He smoothed back her damp hair with loving hands. "You were greedy," he whispered softly, and kissed her.

"I couldn't stop," she confessed. She laughed wickedly, secretively. "You are very sexy."

He nibbled her lower lip. "So are you, *mi esposa.*"

"As first times go," she said with demure pleasure, "that was unbeatable."

"I could return the compliment." He searched her eyes. "We are one, now, completely. Man and wife. One body. One soul."

She touched his mouth and felt his lips purse against her fingers. "I love you so much," she whispered huskily. "Are you sure...?"

"*Querida!*" He sounded shocked. His mouth brushed hungrily all over her face. "How could you doubt what I feel for you now, or do you think such exquisite lovemaking is commonplace between couples?"

"Isn't it?"

He drew her close and kissed her tenderly. "It is not. We loved," he whispered. "Look."

His hand smoothed along her body, which was still intimately joined to his, and felt her ripple with the pleasure. "This is what it means to marry and become part of another person. It isn't the physical act of joining alone, although this is exquisite and beautiful. It is the oneness of mind, heart and soul as well." He looked into her eyes hungrily. "I have never known this with anyone else," he said emphatically. "Only with you."

She relaxed, feeling his possession of her increase.

She moaned, because the pleasure came singing back. "I love you," she said softly.

"As I love you, my heart," he whispered, and kissed her, feeling her body warm and kindle under him. His hand gently stilled the sensuous motion of her hips. "But now you must rest. I won't overtire you, regardless of the endless delight I find in your sweet body."

She sighed and smiled up at him. "Spoilsport."

"Not at all." He chuckled, moving gently away from her. He drew her against his side and pulled the covers over them with a long, weary sigh. "Sleep, for a little while. And when you are rested, we can start again."

Her heart jumped and he felt it under his hand. He laughed, too. "How strong it beats, for a heart that was so badly broken."

"Not broken any longer," she said, correcting him. "Strong and faithful and devoted to you."

"As it should be. What a marvelous future we have to look forward to, Noreen—a shared pleasure in each other's lives and so much in common. Eventually, if God wills, a houseful of children as well." He sighed with sheer joy. "My cup overflows with joy."

"So does mine." She curled into his body and closed her eyes. Somehow, all the bad memories had fled, leaving only the promise of the years ahead. Her hand flattened on his chest, feeling the strong beat of his own heart. "I never dreamed of such happiness."

"Nor I." His arm contracted and he kissed her forehead gently. "Try to sleep now. We have all the time in the world for intimate discoveries and mutual pleasure. You are tired, and I must take great care of you."

She smiled drowsily. "And when you need it, I'll take great care of you." Her eyes closed. "What a wonderful Christmas it's going to be."

He smiled, too. "I'll tie you up with ribbon and put you under the tree, my heart, because you are the best present I ever expect to get."

She laughed softly, nuzzling closer. "I love you."

Outside the curtained window, a light rain was falling. But louder than its faint patter on the windowpanes was the strong beat of Ramon's heart and the metallic whisper of her own. She thought that life could hold no greater pleasure than Ramon in her arms. Her broken heart was truly mended.

*   *   *   *   *

A Long Tall Texan Summer
is also available this month.
Three brand new TEXAN LOVERS
in a special anthology from Diana Palmer—
no sane woman could resist!

COMING NEXT MONTH

NOBODY'S CHILD Ann Major

Children of Destiny

Cutter Lord had always secretly loved his brother's wife, Cheyenne, but her loyalties had been to her husband and son. Then her husband was murdered and her child kidnapped. Now Cutter had to rescue her son; after all, he was the boy's father...

JOURNEY'S END BJ James

The Black Watch

Merrill Santiago had retreated to Ty O'Hara's isolated ranch for some peace and quiet... Instead, the beautiful agent found Ty to be the most dangerous man she'd ever met because he threatened to tear down all her defences.

HOW TO WIN (BACK) A WIFE Lass Small

Tyler Fuller still loved his ex-wife, Kayla, and, having grown tired of spending the long, cold nights alone, he vowed to win her back. But Kayla wanted to take things slow...and Tyler was amazed to discover just how good slow could be...

THE BRIDAL SHOWER Elizabeth August

Always a Bridesmaid!

When Michael Flint learned that Emma Wynn was about to marry another man, he was determined to stop her. She'd turned down his proposal before, but Michael *would* get his 'yes' this time...

LONE STAR KIND OF MAN Peggy Moreland

Wives Wanted!

Years ago, Reggie Giles had loved Cody Fipes...and begged him to run away with her. But Cody had said no and gone off to seek his fortune. Now they're both back and Cody doesn't want to let Reggie go—ever again!

ANOTHER MAN'S BABY Judith McWilliams

Ginny Alton had agreed to impersonate her cousin and travel thousands of miles with her cousin's baby. On arrival, Ginny was met by Philip Lysander who decided to pretend to be the baby's father...and Ginny's lover...

On sale from 22nd May 1998

COMING NEXT MONTH FROM

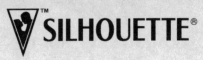 SILHOUETTE®

Sensation

A thrilling mix of passion, adventure and drama

MIND OVER MARRIAGE Rebecca Daniels
LOVING MARIAH Beverly Bird
PRIME SUSPECT Maggie Price
BADLANDS BAD BOY Maggie Shayne

Intrigue

Danger, deception and desire

ANGEL WITH AN ATTITUDE Carly Bishop
FATHER AND CHILD Rebecca York
THE EYES OF DEREK ARCHER Vickie York
STORM WARNINGS Judi Lind

Special Edition

Satisfying romances packed with emotion

ALISSA'S MIRACLE Ginna Gray
THE MYSTERIOUS STRANGER Susan Mallery
THE KNIGHT, THE WAITRESS AND THE TODDLER Arlene James
THE PRINCESS GETS ENGAGED Tracy Sinclair
THE PATERNITY TEST Pamela Toth
JUST JESSIE Lisette Belisle

On sale from 22nd May 1998

Karen Young

Good Girls

When they were good...

Jack Sullivan is an ambitious and painful presence in the lives of three prominent Mississippi women. He made Suzanne a prisoner of violent memories, used Taylor as a lonely trophy wife and drove Annie's mother to suicide. When Jack is murdered, each wonders who finally pulled the trigger...

"Karen Young is a spellbinding storyteller."
—Romantic Times

MIRA®

1-55166-306-6
AVAILABLE NOW IN PAPERBACK

DEBBIE MACOMBER

The Playboy and the Widow

A confirmed bachelor, Cliff Howard wasn't prepared to
trade in the fast lane for car pools. Diana Collins lived life
hiding behind motherhood and determined to play it
safe. They were both adept at playing their roles.
Until the playboy met the widow...

"Debbie Macomber's stories sparkle with love and laughter..."
—*New York Times* bestselling author, Jayne Ann Krentz

MIRA®

1-55166-080-6
AVAILABLE NOW IN PAPERBACK